I0629715

kt webb

THE
EVOLVED

book one

the new era saga

Other Titles:

The New Era Saga (Young Adult Superhero)
Growing Hope (book two)
Choosing Eternity (book three)

Chronicles of Alderwood (YA Fantasy)
Mark of Destiny (book one)
Mark of Fate (book two)
Mark of Darkness (coming in 2021)

Chicago Love Stories (Contemporary Romance)
Hard Habit to Break
Stay the Night
You're the Inspiration
Along Comes a Woman (coming soon)

Anthologies
From Now On: The Last Words Anthology (Dystopian)
Side Effects of Progress

Standalone Novels
Knights of Riona (YA Fantasy)
All I Ask (Contemporary Romance)
To Blake, With Love (Contemporary Romance)
Character Development (coming soon)

Children's:
The Very Brave Knight
Adventures at Bedtime (coming soon)

Cover Design & Branding by:

Emily Wittig of Emily Wittig Designs & Photography

Copyright – 2014 by Kathleen Webb

Editors: Debbie Richardson, Jennifer Sell

This book is a work of fiction. Any references to historical events, folklore, mythology, people, or places are used fictitiously. All other names, characters, places, and incidents are products of the author's imagination, and any similarities to actual events, locations, or persons, living or dead, are entirely coincidental.

All rights are reserved. No part of this book may be reproduced or used in any way without the express written consent of the author.

ISBN 13: 978-0692307731
ISBN-10: 0692307737
BISAC: Fiction / Fantasy / Paranormal

LCCN: 2014918966

Chapter One:
Thatcher

Thatcher Kline was a freak. Or at least he always thought of himself as one. He often wondered how it would feel to be like other boys his age. To have a happy home, to go to school on a regular basis, to never live on the street, or eat out of garbage cans. But he knew his life was destined to be different. From the day he was placed with his first foster family, he knew his life would be complicated. He had no parents, no siblings, and no friends. All he had was an uncanny ability to create and control fire.

He didn't want anyone to know his secret. He was too ashamed and consumed by guilt to do anything but try to ignore it for most of his life. But sometimes he played with it. Sometimes he used it to help him or to keep warm when he found himself sleeping outside after another escape from a foster home or orphanage, which he would probably find himself doing again in the very near future. He had been back in state custody for a week after his most recent escape. His caseworker, Mrs. North, had picked him up at eight that morning for another meeting with another family to be placed in another foster home. She was the one who picked him up from the police station the night his parents died so many years ago. She was the one who picked him up from the police station every time he did something stupid.

The Evolved

"Look, Thatcher, this family is your last chance." The social worker tried to touch his hand, but he pulled away.

He was too absorbed in thought. Maybe they'll finally let him go, so he won't have to go through foster home after foster home, month after month. He was going to be eighteen in seven months, so why didn't they just give up?

"When are you going to realize I just don't care?" he snapped.

"I don't believe that at all. And deep down, I don't think you do either." She looked at him for a moment more, and then looked back at his colossal placement folder with a frustrated sigh.

Thatcher felt tears stinging his eyes as he remembered the reason his life had turned out this way. But he couldn't allow himself to think about that anymore, so he looked up at Mrs. North. She was more like family to him than any of the foster homes he'd been placed in through the years. In fact, family was a foreign concept to him at this point, so he turned and looked out the window.

Mrs. North was talking, but he wasn't listening. He'd turned his attention to the billboard across the street. He smirked as he lit the O's on fire in the word hemorrhoid, and let a single hoot of laughter escape him when the people on the street began to point.

"Is there something funny about what I said?" the social worker asked incredulously. "I don't think there's anything funny about you having to finish your seventeenth year out at an orphanage instead of in a foster home."

Thatcher was brought back to reality. He had made up his mind. He would let them place him with this last foster family, then he would take off on his own the first chance he found. He knew Mrs. North would be disappointed in him, but he was too detached to care.

"Ok, you're right, this isn't funny. I'll behave myself and try to fit in with this new family. When do I move in with them?"

"Well, they're waiting in the interview room. They're a very nice family, and very well-off. They've even discussed the possibility of adopting you. They're a bit quirky, so try to be understanding." She gave him an encouraging smile as she opened the office door and motioned for him to go first.

As they walked down the hall, Thatcher entertained the idea of making a break for it. He didn't know if he could fake a smile and interview with another prospective family he had no interest in staying with. But when they rounded the corner and came to the door, he caught himself mid-step as he stared at the couple waiting for him.

The man was tall and menacing, and his bleach-blond hair and nearly-colorless eyes seemed to prove he wasn't someone to be messed with. The woman was short, with her chestnut hair pulled back into a tight bun. They were smiling at him, but something wasn't right. Mrs. North didn't seem to notice because she beamed back and introduced him.

"Mr. and Mrs. Raleigh, this is Thatcher Kline."

The Evolved

"We're so pleased to meet you, Thatcher. We have been looking for you for a long time," Mrs. Raleigh said, then seemed to realize the irregularity of what she'd said and furrowed her brow.

"What my wife means is we've been looking for a boy like you for quite some time now. You see, we've been searching for a child to complete our family." Mr. Raleigh smiled amiably and nodded at Mrs. North, who blushed and was suddenly very interested in a thread on her shirt.

"So...what, you've been looking for a kid who hasn't made it more than six months in any foster home? Doesn't sound like a very happy home to me," Thatcher said sullenly.

"Oh, quite the contrary, young man. We've been looking for a child we can sense belongs to us. A child who has always been part of our family, but just didn't know it," replied Mr. Raleigh in a speech that seemed very well-rehearsed.

Thatcher wasn't sure what to think as he looked back and forth between the Raleighs and Mrs. North. He took a deep breath and blew it out slowly.

"Alright, if you say so," he replied. "So when do we leave?"

Mrs. North relaxed her furrowed brow and gave Thatcher an encouraging smile. "Well, the Raleighs are ready to take you with them now. If you want to grab your bags from my office, we'll finish the paperwork and you can be on your way!"

Thatcher nodded as he removed himself from the

door frame he'd been leaning on. He headed down the hall to the office, still thinking about his escape plan. He couldn't put his finger on it, but he didn't have a good feeling about the Raleigh's. What had Mrs. North said? They're quirky. He decided that was probably a fair description, although he knew there was something more. Thatcher reached the office and stood in the doorway. He looked around at the desk, the bookshelf, the chairs, and the toy box in the corner. If Mrs. North was the closest thing he had to family, this was the closest thing he had to a home. Thatcher was done feeling sorry for himself, though. He couldn't change his past, but he could make the best of his future. As he picked up his backpack and duffel from the floor next to the chair that should permanently have his butt print in it by now, he started to think about what it would be like to have a real family again. He barely remembered his parents. It had been nearly fourteen years since they died.

He could still hear his mother's screams as the flames rose in his bedroom. When his mother finally broke out the window in his room, his father was already dead. It was like something from a horror film, and at the time, he didn't understand what was happening. She was crying so hard, and her salty tears ran into his hair as she pulled him close and hugged him harder than ever. The smell of burning flesh filled his nostrils and made his stomach turn. She helped him climb out the window, and was almost out herself when Thatcher remembered his best friend in the whole world, his stuffed dinosaur Steggie, was still on his bed. He cried out and tried to climb back into the burning house, but she yelled at him to get to the edge of the street to wait for the fire truck. His mother ran back in to grab the dinosaur. He never saw her again. When her body was recovered, she was halfway out the window, her burnt hands clutching Steggie. They said she died from smoke inhalation. He still had Steggie in his duffel. He was the only link he had to his parents, and he wasn't even real.

He closed his eyes and took a deep breath. If he were gone too long, they'd probably panic. Thatcher's disappearing acts were pretty famous at the Department of Social Services, so they probably had someone guarding every exit. He grinned as he made his way back down the hall, then he arrived outside the interview room. He took a deep breath and savored his last moment before his final attempt at freedom. The door was slightly ajar, and he found himself eavesdropping on a private conversation between his new parents.

"Do you think he remembers the fire?" Mrs. Raleigh asked her husband.

"I'm sure he does, Caprice. The boy was four. We know he is aware of his power. We've been keeping tabs on him for years, but every time we get close, he slips away. The fact that he's had so long to hone his abilities will make this more difficult than I'd like," Mr. Raleigh responded, barely hiding the agitation in his voice.

Thatcher couldn't believe what he was hearing. Who were these people? He strained to hear more but was jolted back when the door swung open, and he found himself face to face with Mr. Raleigh. His face was twisted with fury, but he quickly recovered and put on the mask of a pleasant smile.

"Thatcher! Back already? Mrs. North went to file our paperwork so we can leave. Where would you like to eat for lunch? We'd like to take you out." His smile held more than he cared to share.

Thatcher took the hint and acted like he hadn't heard anything. He gave his best *perfect son* smile and replied, "How about China Palace?"

Once they were in the red sedan, Thatcher began making his plans of escape. His senses were on overload thinking through every impossible scenario, from FBI agents to circus recruiters. He wasn't sure what these two wanted from him, or how they knew about his ability, but it certainly didn't bode well for him. Were they scientists? Or government agents? What interest did they have in him?

Lost in his thoughts, Thatcher was barely aware they'd arrived at their destination. No one had spoken during the ride. He'd seen buildings pass without registering his location, and they'd made turns without him realizing which direction they were headed. How could he have been so stupid? If he didn't know where he was, how could he hope to escape? He looked up and found himself staring at a dilapidated building. It looked like a long-forgotten industrial district, with structures just begging to become unauthorized homeless shelters. This was not China Palace; this was an abandoned warehouse.

"What's going on? Where are we?" Thatcher did his best to keep the fear out of his voice.

The Evolved

"Well, Thatcher, we know you overheard our little conversation, so we don't see a point in continuing this charade." Mr. Raleigh turned around to look at him. He flashed his eerie homicidal murderer smile.

"We know you've discovered your power, and we know you can use it at will. We're hoping this doesn't mean you'll put up too much of a fight." Caprice gave him a stern look.

"Look, I don't know what you guys want, but I don't have any powers. And I'm actually pretty hungry, so I was really hoping we were heading for China Palace." Thatcher tried to play it cool.

"Get out of the car," was all Mr. Raleigh said.

Thatcher didn't move. He decided whatever they had planned, he would definitely disappoint them and put up a major fight. The door opened, then hands reached in and yanked him out by the arm. He found himself standing outside and being roughly shoved against the car.

"Will you at least tell me what this is all about?" Thatcher tried to distract them.

"There's really no point. You won't live long enough for it to be worth my time," Mr. Raleigh replied.

"Then at least tell me your name. I overheard your wife's name is Caprice, but what about you?"

"She's not my wife," Silas spat.

"Whoa, touchy subject?" Thatcher asked, taking a step back.

Caprice got right in his face and breathed a response he would remember for the rest of his life. "You have been our ruin. Your mere existence has destroyed the lives of our brothers and sisters." She turned and looked at the menacing man beside her. "What are you waiting for, Silas?"

Thatcher had heard enough. It was time to get out of there. At least he was an expert at making quick escapes. He closed his eyes and focused on every form of fire he could muster. He let go of years of anger and irritation, and somehow created a volcano, which shot straight up from the ground beneath Caprice. He heard her scream, and Silas cried out in anguish. Thatcher ran away, throwing fireballs in a repetitive volley over his shoulder.

He ran as fast as he could without looking back. Thatcher didn't know where he would go, but he knew it wouldn't be anywhere near here.

Chapter Two:
Hadley

Hadley Callaghan wanted to hide. She couldn't believe what she was seeing, but couldn't bring herself to look away. Her sister was actually flirting with the weird guy at the coffee house. They'd seen him there every day, but he was always alone, with his face buried in a book. Not that there's anything wrong with reading, or frequenting coffee houses—she was a frequenter of coffee houses, and often had her own nose glued in a book—but seriously? This guy?

Cringing at the giggles coming from her twin as she placed a hand on the coffee shop guys' arm, Hadley decided she needed to put a stop to this.

"Whit! Let's get going!" Hadley called a little louder than intended.

Whitley rolled her eyes, but finger waved goodbye to the blushing bookworm.

"You always ruin my fun," said Whitley, pouting as they exited the coffee shop.

"Yeah, well, I didn't appreciate the bile rising up in my throat. Vomit does not make a good coffee creamer," Hadley teased.

Whitley stuck out her tongue, then returned her attention to the Pumpkin Spice Latte in her hand.

Hadley smiled at the passersby, trying to settle into the groove of small-town life. Everyone wanted to say hello, and everyone acted as though they'd known each other all their lives.

Thankful for her favorite brown cardigan, Hadley zipped it up the rest of the way and pulled the sleeves over her hands. The heat from the Cinnamon Latte seemed to intensify when surrounded by the sweater and her hands. Holding the coffee close to her nose, she took a deep whiff and was filled with the nostalgia of everything this time of year brings. The September air was crisp and cool, and the sun was beginning to rise above the old downtown buildings of Benton, providing its warmth to the narrow streets. She was growing to love the sight of the town committee's decorations for their Harvest Festival and smiled thinking about how much fun it would be to join the town in their pumpkin carving and apple cider making. She'd heard it was quite the celebration.

Hadley took in their surroundings. They'd come to this intersection every day for the last five months, and nothing had changed, aside from the decor. Their father chose this area because it made him seem like an average Joe. The voters saw him living on a big ranch, in a small but upwardly mobile town, and automatically related to him. So far, the polls were coming back in his favor, and he looked like a shoo-in for the presidency. The girls weren't sure how they felt about their father's plans to become the next President of the United States. Their mother was gone, so their father was all the family they had. If he became Mr. President, he wouldn't be theirs anymore. The move to Benton had been the first step down a dark and lonely path for the twins.

They wandered over to a bench nestled in between two buildings. Apparently, there had been a building there years ago, but it had since been demolished. Benton loved to display its history, so the sides of the building were now covered in a mural depicting the early settlers as they built up the town. Hadley thought about the people who started Benton. They had been looking for a place to belong—a new home. She wondered what it was like to claim a place as your home; their father's career had led them all over the country, sometimes on a bus. She smiled at the pioneer family in the mural, the mother lifting her child down from the covered wagon.

"Do you ever think about mom?" Hadley blurted out without meaning to.

"Wow, that came out of left field." Whitley looked at her with concern.

"Well, I've been thinking a lot lately about dad and his election chances. I just keep wondering if life would have turned out differently if mom hadn't left." Hadley sighed, knowing this conversation wouldn't go anywhere.

"I don't think so, Had. Dad's been in politics since before we were born. I honestly think if mom were still here, he would have been President before now. The perfect smiling family thing always gets votes." Whitley's response was matter of fact, and Hadley could tell she was still distancing herself from feeling anything about their mother.

"Do you remember her?" Hadley asked quietly.

"I remember her face and her hair. We look just like her. She was beautiful. I think I remember sitting on her lap, playing with her hair while she told us stories," Whitley replied somberly.

"I remember all those things. She used to tell the best stories. I loved that she never needed a book to tell us stories. She had the greatest imagination. Sometimes I wish she would have stayed, and I wonder what would be different now if she had." Hadley blinked away tears as they threatened to escape her eyes.

Whitley reached over and took her hand. "I know, me too. But it doesn't do us any good to think about it. What's done is done."

Hadley nodded in agreement. They lapsed back into silence and sipped their coffee, enjoying the quiet of the morning. She found herself thinking about their mother more every day. On her sixteenth birthday, she decided she would start to look for their mother. She hadn't shared her search with Whitley because she didn't know how she would react. There were so many questions that only their mother could answer. So far, a year of searching had proven fruitless, and she grew more frustrated each time she followed a dead-end lead.

It wasn't the only secret she'd been keeping from her twin. Hadley stole a sidelong glance at her sister. There had always been one constant in her life; she always had Whitley, and Whitley had always been so like her that it seemed they were perfectly in tune.

17

The Evolved

But ever since they hit puberty, Hadley noticed odd things happening to her. If she was really upset, or really happy, or feeling a little blah, the weather seemed to respond to her mood. It was terrifying at first. She really didn't even notice it until Whitley made a joke about her mood swings messing with the atmosphere. Since the discovery, Hadley spent a lot of time learning to meditate. She found that if she put all her focus on whatever feeling was strongest, she could also focus whatever this strange ability was. She had been teaching herself to control it and had gotten to the point where she could call up a breeze at will. And if she focused, she could adjust the temperature indoors or out.

At first, she had been excited to tell Whitley, because she was sure Whitley could do it too. They were identical twins, so everything should be the same. But Whitley never mentioned anything. Hadley didn't want to be responsible for bringing up the only thing that ever made them truly different. She didn't want to lose the only constant in her life.

Sighing, Hadley looked up. The sun was shining and rising in the clear blue sky. Crisp clouds dotted above them like little puffs of cotton. It really was a beautiful day. She was glad she'd learned to control herself, or the weather would reflect the sadness creeping into her heart.

"Hey, there's a new book store opening over there. Let's go check it out," Whitley exclaimed, shocking Hadley out of her thoughts. Leave it to Whit to bring her back to reality and keep her from wallowing in self-pity.

Smiling at the prospect of spending the next few days lost in a good book, Hadley nodded at Whitley. They were free of bodyguards for a few days because their dad was on the campaign trail, traveling the country to meet voters at various speaking engagements. Eric Callaghan had always been overly concerned with their safety and didn't want to leave them alone. But they finally convinced him, at seventeen, that they were old enough to take care of themselves. He only agreed to leave them home alone if they agreed to call him every evening.

She glanced at the sign above the display window, and she could tell it wasn't one of those overdone chain stores. This was an honest-to-goodness old-fashioned book store. A large banner announced The Benton Book Nook was having a Grand Opening Sale. Hadley had noticed workmen coming and going from the space in the months they'd lived here, but there had been no sign until today. She smiled at the thought of immersing herself into the world of ink and paper.

After looking both ways to ensure the road was still deserted, they sprinted across the street, careful to hold their tall lattes steady. She opened the door with a jingle of the bell. They were greeted by the scent of fresh paper and simultaneously inhaled it deeply. The realization made them both giggle.

A young man with black hair and piercing blue eyes poked his head around the corner. "Be with you in a minute!" he called as he disappeared again.

Chapter Three:
Whitley

As soon as Whitley walked into the store, something strange started happening. She could feel a buzzing in the air. It was as if she could feel the energy pulsing around her. She shook her head, writing it off as the anticipation of exploring the book store. It had been so long since she'd been able to go to a physical book store.

As they took the two steps down into the store, Whitley was overwhelmed at the magnitude of books. Usually, if it wasn't a chain store, they only had a few books on hand, and you'd have to wait to order anything they didn't normally carry. But just by sweeping her eyes from left to right, she could tell she would be hard-pressed to find something they didn't carry. The exterior walls were lined with rows of beautiful mahogany bookshelves, with more bookcases jutting out from the walls, creating a narrow hallway of books. Whitley began to wander down the aisle and was surprised to find one of the small nooks created by the interior bookshelves held a fireplace with big leather couches around it. Across from the couches, the sales counter wrapped around a glass case filled with old hardbound books, which she imagined were first editions. It felt like a small library.

She wanted to see how deep the sales floor went, so she headed toward the travel section in the back. When she came to the end of the store sales floor, she found a black metal stairway leading up to a loft. It was roped off with a "do not enter" sign. Curiosity almost got the best of her as she reached for the hook on the chain. Shaking her head, she turned and headed back to take a closer look at some of the sections. She decided there must be thousands of books in the store.

She stopped in the travel section and began perusing the books, looking for their next vacation spot.

"Hey, Had, we should see if dad will let us go to Morocco for Christmas next year. It would be nice to get away and get some sun instead of freezing here!" Whitley called over the rows of books.

The twins may have shared identical DNA, but their personalities had always been like two halves of a whole. Hadley was so different from her. She smiled at the thought of her twin missing out on the festivities of the Christmas season. She knew Hadley was actually looking forward to the coming winter. They hadn't lived in an area that had any snowfall since they were in second grade. Whitley didn't mind not having snow, but she knew for sure her sister was planning to enjoy every inch of snow that fell.

The girls were like mirror images of each other; their thick blond hair and deep brown eyes stood out against fair complexions. But when you look in a mirror, you see the world reversed, and while she shared identical physical features with Hadley, their personalities differed in some major areas. Whitley

The Evolved

had always loved that they were like two halves of one person. She enjoyed having Hadley as her sister and confidante but prided herself on the things that set them apart. It kept things interesting. They were both beautiful inside and out, and their father had instilled humility, along with confidence, in them; they were always caught off guard when someone admired their looks.

Whitley made her way back to her twin, holding the book about Morocco when the man with the black hair stepped in her path carrying a stack of books. Instantly, she felt the buzzing again. They met head-on without stopping, and books fell to the floor in a loud round of thuds. Her coffee spilled, covering her white sweater in pumpkin-scented liquid. As soon as they collided, she felt immense pressure from all angles. She looked around, wondering if they had created a book avalanche. As she reached for the book, the clumsy book store clerk reached a hand out to help her. Whitley felt an intense heat rise in her cheeks. She wanted to melt into the floor, and she was so embarrassed she almost forgot he was there. Her hand touched the book guy's hand, and the heat intensified. The room got dark, and light again, she thought she was about to pass out when the realization hit her, the lights were flickering. She hid her embarrassment easily by adding a little *senator's daughter condescension* to her voice. Her father would have been disappointed in her.

"You should really pay your light bill," she threw at him while the lights continued to flicker.

"Uh . . . what?" Was all he managed to force out.

Whitley pointed up and said, "Your lights. Do they do this often?"

"Oh, no." His eyebrows knit together as he looked up at the ceiling. "In fact, I've owned this building for three years, and it's never happened before."

"You own this place?" Hadley asked, coming up behind him.

"Yeah, Kerr Mason, at your service." He made a little bow and grinned. The light seemed to sparkle in his eyes.

"Hadley Callaghan and the klutz you ran into is my sister Whitley."

"Callaghan, huh? As in Eric Callaghan? Senator Eric Callaghan? The presidential candidate?" Kerr asked.

"Yep, that's our dad. Mr. President himself," Whitley responded with just a hint of venom in her voice.

"Soft spot, huh?" he stage whispered to Hadley.

She nodded and giggled a little. Whitley rolled her eyes at her sister. She couldn't believe Hadley hadn't grabbed her hand and dragged her from the store. That's what she usually did when she caught Whitley in situations she found embarrassing. She noticed Hadley narrowing her eyes at her, and she wondered if her sister could sense how flustered she was.

"Whit, we should probably get going. I'm sure Kerr has to call an electrician or something to get this fixed." Hadley looked around uncomfortably.

Kerr nodded and started to head to the back room

when the jingling of the bell alerted him to another customer. The three of them turned to see who had come in but couldn't see anyone. The flickering lights made it hard to focus on anything. As Kerr tried to pass the girls to offer his assistance to the person who'd entered, he stumbled over one of the books still strewn across the floor. Whitley instantly reached out to steady him. As soon as she made contact with him again, the lights instantly grew steadily brighter.

"Must have fixed themselves," Kerr said as he grinned sheepishly at Whitley. She noticed he had the tiniest specks of green in his clear blue eyes, and having him this close to her sent a shot of pressure through her body again. A moment of familiarity passed through her as if recognizing a kindred soul. The moment was fleeting, but she grinned back as he steadied himself. Her grin relieved the strange sensation all at once like a weight had been lifted off her body.

An explosion filled the air, and glass rained down on them from above. They all ducked and put their arms up protectively. Whitley opened her eyes and found herself in darkness, save for the mid-morning light filtering through the large shop windows.

"What the . . . " Kerr strode to the front of the shop, looking all over for the source of the explosion.

Whitley squatted and touched the ground, looking for the glass that had scratched and cut her arms. Using the light of her cell phone, she found the floor covered in the remnants of fluorescent lights, and the fine powder they leave behind when they burst.

"It's the lights. The light bulbs exploded," she said as

she stood up, holding a chunk of the bulb in the palm of her hand. Dumbfounded, she held it out to Kerr as he came back over to her.

Kerr looked at her in bewilderment. She was speechless. How could this happen? She couldn't help but wonder about the strong energy she felt, and then the place exploded. Using her cell phone for light, she searched the area for an exposed wire that may have shocked her, but there was nothing to explain what happened.

"I'm very sorry about this, ladies, but I'm going to have to close the store until further notice. I really need to clean this mess up and call someone to help figure out what went on here today." Kerr began to usher them out by placing a hand on each of the girls' shoulders.

Whitley felt the rush of heat again, and Kerr pulled his hand back with a shout.

"You must have had some static electricity built up in your sweater. I haven't gotten a shock like that since I tried to stick a paper clip in a light socket." Kerr chuckled.

"Are you sure you don't want help with the cleanup?" Hadley asked.

Whitley shot her twin a sour look as she tried to think of a reason not to stay. Something was off; she didn't know what it was, but she was thoroughly freaked out by everything that had transpired in the last ten minutes.

"Um, sure, if you want to. I'll have to go downstairs to

grab a few flashlights and brooms. I'll be back." Kerr hurried out of sight.

Whitley rounded on Hadley. "What is your problem? We need to get out of here. There is something wrong with this place, with this guy. I have felt so weird since we came in here like the air is vibrating. Then he rams into me, and everything goes all haywire."

Hadley was staring at her as though she'd never seen her before. Whitley was getting irritated and frustrated. She felt like she was going to be next in the explosion line if she didn't get out of there.

"Or maybe it's you. Maybe your hormones are messing with the atmosphere," Hadley replied simply, reminding Whitley of something she'd said years ago.

"Come on, Had. You know that's not possible. Let's get out of here before he comes ba—"

Kerr came up behind her, careful not to touch her again. "Here, I only have two brooms and one flashlight, so do you want to sweep or light the way?"

Whitley hesitated for a moment before grabbing the broom. She didn't want to take any chances with the flashlight.

"Boy, that sure was crazy, huh? I mean, I've never seen anything like it. What in the world would make all those lights explode?" Kerr was chattering like a hyperactive squirrel, and Whitley couldn't help but giggle. There was something different about him, but somehow she knew he wasn't dangerous.

"I can explain these events if you have time." A voice

came from the shelves to their left, causing every cell in her body to stand at attention.

"Who's there?" Kerr held the broom in front of him, protectively stepping in front of the twins.

Whitley smiled. No, he was definitely not dangerous.

A man stepped out of the shadows and into the shaft of sunlight they were standing in. He looked to be in his mid-forties. He wore a brown tailored suit jacket, jeans, and a red button-up shirt. His chestnut hair was beginning to gray, and he beamed at the trio with perfect teeth showing from behind his full beard.

"The name's Dorian. You don't know me, but I've known all of you for a very long time. Excuse me if I seem a little strange. I've been waiting for this day for twenty years."

Whitley felt a chill, wondering if this man was crazy. It was too much of a coincidence for him to show up right after the explosion. She felt Hadley's hand grab hers, and she squeezed back in reassurance. Kerr had tensed. His body looked rigid, and she knew if she could see his face, it would be filled with the confusion she felt.

"I have to say, I'm not surprised you three crossed paths. Of course, I knew Hadley and Whitley would be together, but what a happy coincidence for your father to choose to move you here. Kerr has been here for fifteen years. Ever since his mother married his stepfather." Dorian continued, as if it were completely natural he should know these things, "I imagine you all would like to know who I am, but before we get into the details I would suggest we allow Kerr to contact whomever he must in order to get this place back together."

For a moment, they were all frozen, staring at Dorian as though he were a strange sculpture they couldn't make sense of. Whitley noticed Kerr attempt to start a sentence multiple times, but he failed to utter a sound. Hadley was clinging to her. After a few moments, Dorian cleared his throat, and Kerr threw his hands up in the air and grabbed the phone off the desk. The girls inched closer to him in the gloom, leery of being left alone with Dorian.

Dorian just stood there, smiling with pride. "You ladies really grew into beautiful young women. I knew you would. You look just like your mother."

Chapter Four:
Kerr

Kerr looked over his shoulder suspiciously at the man in his shop as he headed to the phone. He didn't know what was going on, but today had definitely been a weird day. His grand opening sale was just getting started, and he had done fairly well so far. The first few days he had nominal sales and was pleased to see not only locals but tourists enter his shop.

Thinking back to how the last few days had gone made him think about how today started. Kerr had opened the store at nine o'clock and gone about his regular routine. Everything was in its place, so he decided to relax and read a book. It was one of the many great things about owning and working in a book store. He got to spend time doing what he loved. He stepped into the back to grab a bottle of water when the bell jingled to let him know it was showtime.

He knew the moment the girls walked into his store that he had to get to know them. Kerr had never bought into all the stuff about soul mates or fate, but he had always been able to sense things about people. His father called it "reading auras." When Kerr peeked around the counter at the twins, he saw it immediately. More than saw it, he felt it. They were connected somehow. He disappeared into the back room, hoping he could take a moment to breathe before having to face them.

Kerr had spent much of his life avoiding people because the feelings he got from people weren't always positive. He was raised by loving parents—a stay at home mom and a hardworking dad. He didn't have any siblings. His mother always said the moment she looked into his eyes she knew their family was complete. As a child, he spent most of his time with his mother. But his father made sure they spent quality time together whenever he was home. His father was the one who taught him how to read people. He taught Kerr to embrace his gift and not be afraid to use it. It was the most important secret they shared, and the only secret they kept from his mother.

His father meant so much to him, and he soaked up every moment he possibly could with him. Cole was a well-respected historian and often traveled to museums to authenticate various items. One such trip happened to fall over the week of Kerr's sixth birthday, and he'd surprised his son with the opportunity to accompany him.

Kerr remembered the train trip clearly, and he knew they'd taken the train as a special treat. His dad had arranged for them to spend some time with the conductor and have a tour of the entire train. It was one of the best experiences of his life, and one of the last experiences he had with his father. Everything about this trip was built around having fun together, even though his dad had to work.

When they arrived in Chicago, his dad took him to the museum just to look around. They were there late into the night, talking about the adventures they would have had living in different eras. The next morning Cole had to get to work, but this time Kerr got to go too. Kerr enjoyed helping his dad and watching him examine the pieces he had to authenticate. The next day was his birthday, so his dad didn't have to work. He took Kerr to a used book store known for its collection of first editions. Cole knew how much his son loved books. He had taught Kerr to read when he was only four. Kerr loved books, both old and new, but he loved to read a book so worn he could almost see its history as he thumbed through the pages. Of course, as he came to find out later, he really could see the history of objects and locations if he let them speak to him.

His father ended up buying him quite the collection of first editions as a birthday gift. They left the store with two full bags. Kerr was preoccupied with thoughts of the words he would be soaking up on the train ride home. If he had known these were his last moments with his father, he might have been more present. But how could he have known? As they rounded the corner to their hotel, Kerr stopped dead in his tracks. He barely registered the concern in his father's voice when he told him to run. Kerr had come face to face with a man who would haunt his nightmares for years to come.

His father saw the man, and knew instantly he intended to cause them harm. Kerr knew his father must have seen the darkness lurking around the man with fiery red hair and a full beard, and when his dad tensed up and told him to run, he immediately obeyed.

The Evolved

Kerr still couldn't remember how he'd ended up sitting on a bench in the police station. But he remembered his mother's arrival and her tear-stained face. She handed him the bag of books his father had been carrying and stroked his hair. She told him they didn't know what happened. She told him it looked like he'd died instantly. But Kerr knew she was trying to make him feel better. When he had seen the terrifying man, he saw what he was going to do to them.

He saw his father burning to death from the inside out.

He had encountered many "auras" in his life, but he'd never encountered anyone who affected him this way. Kerr closed his eyes and took a deep breath. At least not until the twins came into his store. When he ran into Whitley, he saw bits and pieces of her future, and it included him. He had to find out who they were.

He grabbed the phone and dialed the number to the cleaning service he'd hired. After a brief explanation of what had happened, they agreed to be there in half an hour. He hung up with the cleaners and dialed the electrician he used when he renovated the building. The electrician said he wouldn't be able to work him in until tomorrow. He hung up and sighed. It looked like his grand opening would have to be delayed.

Taking a step out behind the store, he thought about when he collided with Whitley. For a moment, he'd been able to see her as more than she appeared. It was as though he could visualize the power around her, he sensed good and beauty. Not to mention, the brief amount of time Kerr spent with Hadley gave him the same impression. He knew this was not an accidental meeting, but something planned by a higher power.

He headed out to the front of the store again, hoping he could get some answers from the man who'd introduced himself as Dorian.

"Well, the electrician can't come until tomorrow, but the cleaners will be here in about half an hour. So, Dorian, was it? You mind telling us what you want?" Kerr tried to sound older than his twenty-two years.

Dorian chuckled and raised a hand. "Hold the tough guy act, Kerr. It's not necessary. I won't hurt you. In fact, think of me as the kindly old uncle you never knew." He saw this wasn't a good enough response, and continued, "I am not going to cause you any harm. You can trust me. Kerr, look at me closely. What do you see?"

Whitley wrinkled her nose. "What does that even mean?"

Kerr shrugged. He didn't want to share too much before he got to know the girls more. "Look, I'll play along, you're not a bad guy, I get it. I don't know what you think you know about me, but you're scaring these girls."

Hadley and Whitley made offended sounds at the same time.

"We're not scared," Hadley responded with a hint of irritation.

"Right, well, you said you had some explanations, and

we're waiting for them." Kerr looked directly at Dorian for the first time. He looked into his eyes and saw a faint spark. He knew from that spark that Dorian was telling the truth. He could trust him. This man had done a lot of good in his life, and he was strong. Something was lurking below the surface, but he couldn't quite get a read on it.

Dorian nodded. It was as if he knew what Kerr had just discovered. He found it unnerving to feel as though someone could read him as easily as he could read them.

"Okay, I can't speak for the girls, but I want to hear what you have to say." Kerr gestured to the back of the store. "We can go up to my loft. It's on a different breaker, so it's possible it was unaffected by the blast. In any case, it has huge windows, so there's probably enough natural light to see."

"Wait a minute. We're not going anywhere with you. We literally just met you both today. All we know about you is you own this place. And all we know about him is he's creepy," Whitley said a little louder than she intended.

Dorian and Kerr exchanged a glance. Kerr shrugged helplessly. He knew he wouldn't be able to tell the twins they could trust them. What proof could he offer without freaking them out? Dorian seemed to be thinking the same thing.

"Hadley, how has the weather been lately?" Dorian asked smugly.

Hadley's mouth hung open. Whitley looked at her in

confusion. Hadley quickly regained her composure and swallowed hard.

"Okay, we'll go with you," she said, taking Whitley's hand and dragging her along behind her.

Kerr led the way to the back of the store and unhooked the chain on the stairs leading up to his loft. He stood back to allow the group to go ahead of him. When they reached the hallway at the top, he headed to unlock the door. After everyone filed in and took their seats around his dining room table, they sat waiting for Dorian to begin his story.

Chapter Five:
Dorian

"My story begins many years ago, with a race of people who have been in existence since the dawn of time. They've been known by many names, and appear throughout history. There have been many theories about their many names, but the connection hasn't been made that they are all the same people. Those of us who know their story call them the Old Immortals, but you may know them as Nephilim, Emites, Rephaites, Anakim, Greek gods, Roman gods, Norse gods, Egyptian gods, and most recently, the Mayans."

He listened as the sharp intake of breath echoed around the table.

"Through the years, they discovered they had been given a gift from their Creator. The Old Immortals were each gifted with unimaginable powers and immortality. It was because of these gifts the humans were convinced they were gods. But the Old Immortals knew that no matter what the mortals believed, there had only ever been one Creator. The Creator saw the good they could do for humankind. The Old Immortals could teach them and help them to mold their primitive settlements into civilizations. Any time in history when societies made great advances in areas such as science, technology, or architecture, the Old Immortals were responsible. Some humans feared them, but some embraced them. If they were met with fear or reproach, the Old Immortals left peacefully. In all the places that received their assistance, they could only stay for a few hundred years."

Kerr looked at him and laughed. "Only a few hundred years? Only?"

Dorian smiled and continued, "They finally decided to step away from humankind to develop their abilities and separate themselves from society, and they settled in an area that was far from civilization. But it didn't take long for them to be found. No matter where they went, it seemed as though humans were drawn to them like moths to a flame. Soon, villages sprang up in the areas surrounding them. The humans made sacrifices to them and followed their word as law. And so they became the parents of many great civilizations."

So far, Dorian had the undivided attention of his audience. He was pleased to discover they didn't wear expressions of irritation and didn't seem to be looking at him like a mad man. He cleared his throat and continued.

"One of the many forms of sacrifice was for the villagers to offer a young virgin. At first, they would kill the poor girls, because it was believed that through giving something so precious, they would prove they were true servants of their gods. When the Old Immortals discovered the purpose behind these sacrifices, they tried to explain a blood sacrifice was not something they wanted but something they abhorred. The villagers did not understand. So finally the Old Immortals requested the virgins be delivered to the foot of the steps of their grand pyramid, alive."

He could see from Hadley's eyes a realization was beginning to dawn at the back of her mind, but he was pleased she didn't yet voice her thoughts.

"You see, years before, the Old Immortals had discovered they were unable to conceive children amongst themselves. They believed the gifts they'd been given were meant to be shared, so they wanted to produce children so their legacy would continue to grow. Each year, as a virgin was delivered to their door, she would be wed to one of the Old Immortal men. And each time one of these marriages occurred, a child would be conceived from their union. The young wives were treated as queens because, without them, it would not have been possible to grow their race. The joy they felt at being able to produce children was unimaginable. After the first child was born, there was a huge celebration to welcome him to the world. The celebration was short-lived, however, as sadly, his mother died in childbirth. This was fairly common in those days, so while they were deeply aggrieved, they didn't think there was harm in continuing to produce children with mortal women. When each of them had a human wife in different stages of pregnancy, it became clear the mothers would not survive to deliver the children of the Old Immortals. For the first time in their history, the Old Immortals found themselves divided. Some believed they should stop trying to conceive children, and that maybe it wasn't in the plans their Creator had for them. Some believed the Creator wouldn't have allowed a child to come at all if it wasn't meant to be, and the death of the wives was just collateral damage."

He heard a sharp intake of breath come from Whitley but saw the expressions of the others, indicating they were ready to hear more. He sighed and decided to continue.

"Those who decided it was wrong no longer took wives and were thankful for the children they were blessed with. The others continued to take wives and allowed them to bear the pain and suffering of long, drawn-out deaths. Because the mothers died at the birth of their child, the barren women of the Old Immortal race raised the children as their own. As the children grew, it was clear they favored the father's side of the family. They developed special abilities and stopped aging when they reached young adulthood. They also discovered the new generation they'd fathered was not cursed with the same inability to bear children as they were. Their daughters were able to marry and produce healthy children without dying in the process."

Dorian looked at them as they hung on every word like children at storytime. It was the best possible reaction to the information he shared.

"As the years went on, the Old Immortals began to feel weaker. They didn't understand what was happening. Their children and grandchildren, and great-grandchildren, and so on, were stronger with each generation, but they were weakening. Some of the Old Immortals felt this was evolution—they had served their purpose, and their Creator was allowing them to fade until they were no more. But others felt what was happening was unfair. Look what they'd accomplished, this couldn't be their fate. Those who couldn't accept what was happening began finding ways to reclaim some of their power. They discovered that if they killed their descendants, some of their power would revert back to them. Many succeeded in doing just that before the Old Immortals, who fell on the side of evolution, realized what was happening. Slowly, their progeny began to disappear, until only a handful remained."

He saw looks of concern on the faces in front of him. He knew they would start to realize what he was driving at, but he didn't want them to think too hard on it just yet.

"Now is the part that will seem less like a grim bedtime story, and more like a reason to lock me up in an asylum. Before I go further with the story, I must tell you, I am far older than I appear. I am one of those Old Immortals, my brothers, sisters, and I have walked this earth for thousands of years, and our lives are coming to an end. Some of us have already faded away, but a few of us remain."

Dorian noticed Kerr seemed to be fighting an inner battle, so he smiled kindly at him for not interrupting. Hadley looked as though she had been crying, and Whitley sat with her eyes wide, clinging to every word he said. He quietly wondered how they would react to the next part of his story.

"I have three brothers and one sister remaining. Two of my brothers are the type who seek out their

The Evolved

descendants and kill them to regain their power—their names are Silas and Absalom. So far, they have murdered over a thousand just between them, and when they finished killing the descendants in their direct line, they decided they could regain power by killing their nieces and nephews. My sister, Tahlia, my brother, Romulus, and I have been keeping close tabs on you because you are what is left of our descendants. You are what we have come to call the Evolved. All of you have been under our protection for your entire lives. Unfortunately, you have all lost the parent holding the bloodline linking you to us. My final descendant shares all of my power, and it is just a matter of time before I fade away completely. Her name is Nora Lowell."

"Wait a minute, our dad is a senator. Our mom ran out on us when we were little. What makes you think we're connected to this?" Hadley asked.

"Hadley, you and your sister are actually a very special case. Your mother is the only remaining female of our race. You are the only children ever born to a female Old Immortal. You are also a rarity because you are the only set of twins ever born into our family. She had to leave in order to protect you. Having her around was like a homing beacon to our brothers, and they would love to get their hands on you."

Hadley was crying openly. "How can we possibly know what you're saying is true? It's so hard to even attempt to believe this craziness. Our mother is gone. I've been looking for her for over a year."

Whitley looked hurt and confused. "You've been

searching for mom and haven't told me? I would have helped you, Had!"

Dorian smiled and gently placed a hand on each girl's shoulder. "Your mother couldn't use her real name when she married your father. You have undoubtedly been searching for Lia Foster. She created a name when she fell in love with your father. There is no Lia Foster. Your mother is one of my kind. Her name is Tahlia. Your mother is at my house right now."

"Whoa whoa whoa! What are you talking about? I don't believe this. Look, I don't know Hadley and Whitley well, but I don't think it's right to mess with them like this," Kerr said incredulously.

Dorian sighed. "I don't know you'll believe me until you all see for yourselves. Would you all be so kind as to accompany me to my estate? It's just outside of town."

"Yeah, I don't think that's a good idea. I've seen one too many horror films to know what comes next." Whitley glanced at Hadley nervously.

Dorian laughed, and his laughter filled the small loft. He knew it wouldn't be easy to convince the girls to go with him, but if he gained Kerr's trust, he was certain the girls would follow suit.

"Kerr, I know you can see that there will be no foul play. I invite you to search my past for any indication that I may intend to bring harm to any of you," Dorian said warmly.

He closed his eyes and felt the slightest tug in his mind. He knew Kerr was starting to skim the surface of his intentions. He relaxed and sent him images of the protection they'd all been unaware of for so long.

"I think we can trust him. I will go with you, Dorian," Kerr answered finally.

After much discussion, the girls came to the same conclusion and decided to go with him. The relief Dorian felt was immense because he wanted them to choose to come under his protection. They had to choose if they wanted to survive.

Chapter Six:
Thatcher

Heading down the alley behind the coffee shop, Thatcher began to shudder at the chill seeping into his bones. He looked around to make sure the coast was clear before closing his eyes and focusing on the Earth's core. He could feel the heat rising from his feet through the rest of his body. A slow smile spread across his face as he felt the warmth reach through his farthest extremities.

Thatcher allowed himself to sit down against the wall. He had been running for months. All he knew was he'd passed three state lines and hadn't eaten in days.

He broke the connection between his body and the heat source he used most often while sleeping outside. He was thankful for his ability because without it he would have frozen to death years ago. When he was twelve, he decided to stop waiting around for a "forever family" and take matters into his own hands. That was when he started running away from every foster home Mrs. North placed him in. Since running away from Silas, he was allowing himself to think more about his past and was starting to remember the painful event that brought him to Mrs. North in the first place.

Thatcher hadn't had a family since he was four. His

parents were the picture-perfect example of a loving family; they loved each other, and they loved him. Sometimes, when he closed his eyes, he could remember bits and pieces about his life before he became a ward of the state. He could see his mother smiling at him, or his father pretending not to see him behind the curtain during a game of hide-and-seek. He could remember their small two-bedroom house with yellow siding and blue shutters. And he could remember the fire.

The first time Thatcher discovered his abilities, he was in his bedroom, on his fourth birthday. He had tried to play with his new baseball in the house and was in his room, thinking about his actions. He almost broke the lamp his mother said came from her grandmother. He remembered thinking it wasn't fair because he didn't even get any cake. And he remembered being almost asleep when he heard his parents coming down the hall. He propped himself up on his elbows, sure he was about to get a good talking to, but was greeted by his smiling parents, holding a piece of cake with a candle on top. They sang "Happy Birthday" to him, and he watched the flame dance in the dim light of his room.

After that, things became a blur. It was like a skipping DVD—some scenes played clearly, others repeated themselves, and still, others were missing completely. He could remember thinking the flame was pretty, and he liked watching it waver as his parents' breath blew it with their song.

His next memory was of the paper plate catching on fire and his mother dropping it as she cried out in alarm. Thatcher remembered his father yelling words he'd gotten in trouble for repeating days before. He remembered the panic set in as the fire suddenly seemed to engulf the whole room. It seemed the more he panicked, the stronger the blaze became.

He still didn't know what exactly happened after that. He knew his parents died, and he knew it was his fault. He was told his mother almost made it out, but his father didn't stand a chance. He often held Steggie and wondered if he had traded his mother for a stupid stuffed dinosaur. Sometimes, when he had nightmares, he saw his father completely engulfed in flames, desperately trying to extinguish them. Thatcher had no way of knowing if it were a memory or just a terrifying vision he'd conjured up as a result of the stories police and social workers told him.

At the age of seventeen, there was only one thing Thatcher Kline knew for sure; he was alone. His parents were dead, he was a freak and felt withdrawn from the world because of the fear he held that his ability would kill everyone he let himself care about.

Thatcher took a deep breath and continued down the alley, feeling the warmth slowly wear off. It was unseasonably cold for September, even in the Midwest. He wasn't sure what made him decide to head to this small town; it probably had something to do with the fact that he'd never been to South Dakota, and therefore, none of the police or social workers knew to look for him. He smiled at the thought of being free. It wasn't a feeling he knew, after spending so many years being treated like property.

The alley spilled out onto one of the main roads in the

town. He hadn't bothered to learn the names of either because he wasn't sure he would be staying. He began to look for a place to rest while he considered his next step. He sat down on a bench and found himself staring at a mural. From the building-sized painting, he discovered the town must be called Benton.

The quiet morning was interrupted by the jingle of a bell. Thatcher looked up to discover four people leaving a building, which proclaimed itself as the Benton Book Nook. He watched them for a moment, then leaned his head back on the bench and shut his eyes.

"Well, Thatcher, just in time! This is all turning out so well!"

Thatcher snapped his eyes open and found himself staring at the group of people who had just come out of the book store.

"My name is Dorian. This is Kerr, Hadley, and Whitley. If only you'd gotten here a few hours ago, you could have heard the story with them." Dorian smiled.

Thatcher raised an eyebrow and looked at the man who had just introduced himself as Dorian. He realized his mouth was hanging open, and quickly shut it with a shake of his head.

"I'm sorry, how do you know me?" Thatcher asked, feeling suspicious after his experience with Silas and Caprice.

"Oh, we'll get to that. You might as well come along with us, young man." Dorian smiled kindly and gave Thatcher an appraising look. "You look just like him.

It's terrifying, really."

The others looked to be about his age, or maybe a little older. They looked just as confused as he felt, but he thought he'd better play along for now. He nodded at each of them, studying their faces for the first time. The guy who was introduced as Kerr looked like the kind of guy that girls seemed to love these days; he had dark, messy hair and looked like a Greek sculpture. At first glance, Thatcher thought he could probably take the guy down if he needed to, but then he noticed the muscular arms and shoulders under his striped polo shirt.

The girls were identical in every way, apart from their clothes. They had shiny, long golden hair and eyes the color of chocolate. He noticed the girls stayed close to the Greek god and held hands in an attempt to stay together. He eyed them warily.

"Um, look, I don't know who you are or how you know me, but I'm not going anywhere with you," Thatcher retorted.

Dorian smiled and looked directly at him. "I've just told these three they're descendants of an ancient race of immortals and have special abilities, and they're still coming with me. As a matter of fact, you already know about your abilities. Why don't you show them so they can be reassured? I'm really not filling them with *hot* air."

Thatcher raised his eyes to meet Dorian's. A silent agreement passed between them. He didn't know who this man was, but he'd gotten himself out of more dangerous situations. And he was interested in hearing the same story he'd told the others. Thatcher nodded his head and took a deep breath. He snapped his fingers, and a flame came to life in his hand. Whitley cried out and tightened her grip on her sister. Hadley uttered a few choice words, and Kerr looked dumbfounded.

"Holy crap," was all Kerr managed to utter as he leaned away.

"Thatcher discovered his ability on his own when he was four. And from what I saw today, Whitley is beginning to discover hers. You each have a natural tendency to use your ability but haven't realized your full potential yet. Kerr, you have a knack for reading the intentions of others, and much more. Hadley, I know you've been working on your control over weather. And Whitley, your display with the exploding lights shows your control over matter and the energy around you. This is just the beginning of what you can do. Even Thatcher has only scratched the surface of his abilities. You each have inherited the main ability of your ancestor, but have also been imbued with the abilities of my brethren who have faded away."

They sat in silence for a few minutes. A look of concern crossed Thatcher's face.

"Do you know a Silas or a Caprice?" Thatcher asked with a furrowed brow.

"Yes. I know you had the unfortunate experience of meeting them. However, Caprice did not survive your encounter. She was incinerated. You see, Old Immortals can only be killed by The Evolved. And whether you knew what you were doing or not, your pyrotechnics managed to take down one of our enemies," Dorian responded.

"How can you talk so nonchalantly about your siblings? I can't imagine what I would do if something happened to Hadley. She's part of me," Whitley said in a very small voice.

Dorian laughed. "You have to forgive my terminology. The members of my race are not actually my brothers and sisters in the literal sense. But we have been together for so long we call each other by those familial terms. So, they are all essentially my family."

Thatcher had already made up his mind. He was going to follow Dorian. If these others had abilities like him, and if he had more abilities to discover, maybe he would finally find a place he fit in.

"Well, are we going somewhere or what?" Thatcher asked.

Dorian nodded. "Yes, let's get going, my car is over there. I think we can all squeeze in. We'll be at my home just in time for supper."

The group followed Dorian to his car and literally had to squeeze into the lime green Ford Focus. Thatcher sat in the front seat. As the youngest and newest addition to the Evolved, he felt like a bit of an outcast. They drove for a little while in silence, but Thatcher could feel the tension in the air.

"So, Thatcher, it's a bit strange that you suddenly showed up here," said Kerr.

"Trust me, it wasn't sudden. I've been on the run for

months. After my run-in with Mr. and Mrs. Psycho, I just kept going. I didn't want to get caught, and I was convinced they were following me," Thatcher said.

"Where were you before?" Hadley asked curiously.

"I grew up in Illinois, and that's where I was until about a month ago when I was adopted by the parents from hell," Thatcher responded.

"So you made it across three states in a month. Have you been hitchhiking or walking?" Kerr asked.

"A little of both. For a while, I even traveled with a carnival, and I ran the Ferris wheel. It got me across Wisconsin in no time," Thatcher said.

Thatcher turned in his seat to look at his new friends. He decided this would be a good time to tell them what happened to his family. He looked at each of them and hesitated. He didn't want them to have a negative opinion of him already, but it would happen sooner or later, and he'd rather not have the pretense of friendship beforehand.

"I gotta tell you guys why I was a ward of the state." Thatcher took a deep breath and continued, "My parents are dead. And I killed them."

Dorian spoke up. "Thatcher, don't ever look at it like that. You didn't know what you were doing."

"You knew? You knew this whole time, and you never came to find me? I am seriously screwed up because I killed my parents, and you could have kept me from getting this way?" He felt the heat rise in his cheeks and had to control himself.

Dorian looked at him sadly, shaking his head. "I couldn't. When I learned about you, I realized there was no way I could bring you in. It was best for you if you moved around a lot. You are the last descendant of Absalom. If you'd been in one place, it would have made it too easy for him to find you. It took them fourteen years to get to you in the foster system. I'm sorry, Thatcher, but this was the only way I could have handled this situation."

Thatcher folded his arms like a sullen child. He stared out the window and considered Dorian's words. He was probably right, but Thatcher wasn't going to admit it.

"Can you fill the rest of us in?" Whitley asked.

"My parents died in a house fire that I started. It was my birthday. I was so upset, and when they showed up in my room with cake, the candle was so enticing. The first time I ever manipulated fire, my dad burned to death; I still remember the smell of his burning flesh. My mother almost made it out, but she died getting my stupid stuffed dinosaur," Thatcher responded, barely holding back the tears he'd contained since his first foster home.

"My father was killed with fire too," Kerr said quietly. "I saw it before it happened, but I couldn't stop it."

Thatcher and Kerr locked eyes for a moment, and a feeling of kinship passed between them. Fire was so destructive, but it could also create life. The deaths that affected their lives so deeply had brought them to this day. Without those deaths, they'd never have known who they were, or how their destinies were

The Evolved

intertwined.

Chapter Seven:
Nora

"Alright, Tahlia, would you sit down for one minute?" Nora Lowell shook her head at her aunt, many times removed.

"I can't sit down. Dorian called. They're on their way! I haven't seen my girls in five years, and it was only from a distance. I haven't spoken to them since the night I left. Oh God, what if they can't forgive me?" Tahlia was thousands of years older than Nora, but she always thought it was amazing; she looked like she was only thirty. Her long blond hair surrounded her in thick waves, and her round face was free of wrinkles.

Nora took her aunt by her narrow shoulders and turned her until they were face to face. "They will. It may take some time, but they will understand."

She watched as Tahlia wiped the tears from her cheeks. When she saw Tahlia's moment of insanity had passed, she plopped down in her favorite chair in the library.

Nora sat in quiet contemplation. Everything was about to change. The home she had made with the Old Immortals was about to become home to four others like her. The more she thought about what was coming, the more she found herself feeling apprehensive about meeting the other Evolved. She wasn't sure how they would feel about her.

She was raised by her many times' great-grandfather, Dorian. She grew up knowing about her roots and the truth about her history. She had begun using her abilities at such a young age, and they'd become part of her. But the others were either just learning about it all, or had only begun to learn the extent of their power.

She was especially worried about her potential relationship with Hadley and Whitley. She had gotten to be with their mother since she was eight, but they only got to be with her for five years. Nora had always wanted to meet them because she knew they held such a special place in Tahlia's heart. Since Tahlia had been the only mother figure she'd ever known, she always thought of the twins as her sisters.

Until today, all the stories about the Old Immortals had been at the back of her mind. It was part of her, but it wasn't who she was. Aside from her abilities, she was a completely normal young woman. She had gone to school but was a few grades ahead of other kids her age. She graduated high school at sixteen and completed her college education the previous May. Until a few months ago, she was wondering if she should just move out and start her own life. Now that the other Evolved were coming here, she knew her past was going to become an integral part of her present.

She leaned her head against the oversized micro-suede chair and thought about all the moments that brought her to this day. Her parents had died in a car accident when she was barely a year old, and she didn't have a single memory of them. The police reports and newspaper articles all said it was an accident—an icy road at night. Anyone could lose control of their vehicle. But she knew it was actually her uncles, Silas and Absalom, who were responsible. They had killed so many, and they hadn't realized that by destroying their bloodline, they were actually creating the force that would be their demise.

Through the years, she had grown to understand the journey her ancestors had traveled. She had spent many hours listening to stories about the people and places they molded. Nora was terrified about her part in this process. Her love for Dorian, Romulus, and Tahlia was so strong the thought of losing them was physically painful. Knowing the legacy she and the other Evolved would be bringing to an end was the hardest part of all.

She stared listlessly around the room; Dorian had an incredible library. There were hundreds of books about the Old Immortals. Most of them were written about the myths people had come to believe about the various identities they had through the years. The myths that interested her most were the ones that described the coming of the New Era. Knowing the important role she and the other Evolved would play in the coming months and years caused a knot to form in her stomach. There was only one book off-limits to her. The leather-bound book of prophecies. The cover was worn, but the symbol on the front was there. A pentagon divided into fourths, each with its own design and a three-part circle in the middle. The symbols had always intrigued her. There was a shield with the face of a lion, a single flame, a heart, and a symbol that looked like a roman numeral two. She wasn't allowed to read it. Dorian said she had to receive her prophecy with the other Evolved, but she'd seen it many times.

Silas and Absalom were formidable enemies. They had ruthlessly murdered thousands of their descendants and the descendants of their brethren. Each time they murdered one of their own, they grew more powerful and lost part of who they were created to be. From everything Nora read in Dorian's library, she figured out only the Evolved could stop them. Thatcher had unknowingly proven that when he dealt with Caprice.

"What do you think they're like?" she asked Tahlia.

"Who? My girls?" Tahlia was clearly in her own world.

"No. Well, yes. I mean the other Evolved. Do you think they'll like me? Do you think they'll be willing to work together in this?" Nora looked hopefully at her aunt.

"Well, the fact that they accompanied Dorian here on their own speaks for itself. If they didn't find truth in his words, they wouldn't be on their way here now. Don't worry, Nora, they will love you just like we do." Tahlia smiled.

Nora sighed and repositioned herself in her chair. The more she thought about it, the more her confidence grew. Tahlia was right; they wouldn't be coming if they weren't ready. And she knew now more than ever they needed to be ready.

Silas was furious about losing Caprice, as they knew he would be. He had been with her for too many lifetimes to count. Nora knew he would not let this go. Silas would look at what Thatcher did as yet another reason why they should wipe out all of the Evolved.

Footsteps approached on the polished oak floor. Nora turned to see Romulus wearing his khaki-colored trench coat. He carried his briefcase and pulled his suitcase behind him. When he saw Tahlia and Nora, a smile broke across his face.

"Welcome home, Uncle Romulus!" Nora sang out as she ran to hug her teddy bear of an uncle, and her spirits lifted instantly.

"I'm glad I didn't miss their arrival. Dorian sent me a text to let me know they were coming. He asked that we all be here. It's a good thing I was already on the flight home, otherwise he would have been out of luck!" Romulus shook his head and chuckled.

Nora loved Romulus. He was a big man and quite intimidating, but he was the sweetest man she'd ever met. His dark brown hair and deep blue eyes, combined with his naturally tan skin, gave him an exotic look that made it difficult to determine his ancestry. His wife was the first virgin sacrifice delivered to the temple. He had fallen in love with her the moment he saw her. The story was very sweet.

Originally, the Old Immortals asked for the virgins to be delivered to them so they could keep them from being killed. Romulus was the one to bring her into the temple. He told Nora, at that moment, that he felt complete. None of the women in his race had ever caught his eye. He was one of the few unwed men. But he knew this was the girl for him. Her name was Anu, and to hear Romulus talk about her, Nora was certain she was the most beautiful woman who had ever lived.

Romulus finally worked up the courage to tell her how he felt and was pleased to discover she felt the same. They wasted no time in becoming husband and wife. They spent a few years basking in the love they'd found, and their happiness radiated from them. When they discovered she was expecting a child, it was a miracle. Romulus felt the Creator was smiling down on their union by blessing them in such an amazing way.

But their happiness was short-lived. When it was time for his son to be born, he was devastated to discover his beautiful Anu was gone. Although his brothers continued to marry the virgin sacrifices, Romulus never remarried, and never had another child. But his son went on to have a son, and so on. His descendants were all sons and all only children. The last in the Present Era was Kerr Mason.

"Nora?" She looked up to find Romulus and Tahlia staring at her with concern.

"Oh, sorry, did you say something? I was just thinking about the others again," she said with an embarrassed grin.

Romulus knelt in front of her and pushed her auburn-colored hair out of her eyes. He patted her cheek and said, "Beautiful niece, you have nothing to worry about. You are strong, smart, and loved. The confidence and compassion you display are a testament to your old soul. They will see these things and appreciate them. Even I often forget you are only in your twentieth year. You'll see, Nora. They will love you, just as we do."

"Thank you, Romulus, you can always make me feel better." Nora leaned forward to pull him into a bear hug.

She heard the front door open and the low rumble of her grandfather's voice echoing in the foyer. Nora and Tahlia grinned at each other as Romulus jumped to his feet. He was surprisingly agile for his size.

Nora gave both their hands a reassuring squeeze. She took a deep breath and fell in line behind Romulus and Tahlia. As she walked down the familiar hall, she couldn't help but feel nervous and giddy all at once. They reached the end of the hallway and stood facing the large open kitchen. The breakfast nook was to their right, and the foyer was to the left. They peeked around the corner into the foyer, stacked on top of each other like kids trying to catch a glimpse of Santa on Christmas morning. She heard Tahlia gasp at the sight of her daughters, and felt the pride in Romulus' posture at the sight of Kerr. Nora knew this would be a very emotional day.

Dorian turned and smiled in their direction. "Well, you three might as well come out. I think it's time everyone met."

Together, they came out from behind the wall separating the hallway from the foyer. Nora made sure to keep her distance from Tahlia until she knew how the twins would react.

Chapter Eight:
Hadley

Hadley and Whitley stood together, holding each other. The pain in her chest was indescribable. Her mother hadn't changed a bit in the years since she left. Hadley watched the woman she'd been searching for approach them with tears rolling down her cheeks.

Tahlia looked uncertainly at them and took another step toward them. The girls stared at their mother, trying to hold it together. Hadley had wondered what this moment would be like from the moment Dorian told them her mother would be here. They stood there looking at each other for what seemed like an eternity. She wasn't sure she was ready to forgive her mom just yet, but right now, all she wanted was to wrap her arms around her and feel that she was real.

Hadley let go of Whitley's hand, took a step forward, and collapsed into her mother's arms. Before she knew it, Whitley had wrapped her arms around them both, and they sank to the floor.

She heard the others quietly leave the room, and they huddled on the floor until they were out of tears.

When they finally let go, the twins followed their mother into a sitting room off the entryway. They each took a seat in silence and stared at anything but each other for as long as they could.

The Evolved

"I need you to understand something. The night I left was the worst night of my life. And every day since, I have felt the pain and regret of not being with you. But I know in my heart it was the only decision I could make to keep you safe," Tahlia said, looking out the window.

"I can't speak for Whitley, but I'm not ready to accept that. I don't think it was better to leave, I think it was easier. You left a gaping hole in our family and didn't have the decency to even explain why you left," Hadley choked out.

Whitley came to sit next to her and grasped her hand. Their mother slowly turned to look at them, and her eyes were red and puffy.

"That's not true. I wrote you letters, I sent them to you. I wrote to you both every week! I can't believe Eric didn't give you my letters." Tahlia's face flushed red with anger.

"Leave dad out of this. We are so not playing the blame game here. If you're going to talk about things he did or didn't do, you better make sure it's when he's around to defend himself," Whitley snapped.

"I wasn't trying to blame him for anything. In fact, I don't blame him for not letting you have the letters. But you have to know he wasn't completely innocent in this. He told me to leave." Their mother gave them a pleading look.

Hadley exchanged a questioning look with her sister. What did she mean dad told her to leave? Their father had always painted a picture of abandonment and loss when it came to their mother. Had it all been a ploy to get sympathy votes for his career? Hadley decided it was time to get some answers.

"What do you mean he told you to leave? He always told us you sneaked out during the night without a word," Hadley said without blinking.

"I'm sorry to tell you this, but that is a complete falsehood. You're probably too young to remember, but the month before I left, things started getting pretty rocky in our marriage. I had finally worked up the nerve to tell your father my story. I was concerned because I noticed you were both starting to show signs of the power you would grow to have. Whitley, you kept showing up in our bedroom when the door was locked from the inside, and every time Hadley threw a tantrum, a freak thunderstorm would hit. I knew these things were connected to you both because those are the abilities you inherited from me." Their mother paused to look at them.

"How did I manage that?" Whitley asked.

Hadley felt a pang of regret as she saw the strain on her twin's face. She knew this was hitting Whitley hard because, before today, she had no clue these things were even possible.

Hadley and Whitley listened as their mother explained.

"You have to understand that you are the only children ever born to a female Old Immortal. I'm sure Dorian has told you our history, so you must know you are truly unique. When you were born, I knew it would only be a matter of time before Silas and Absalom found you and took you from me. They wouldn't want to kill you, they'd have wanted to use you. You are a miracle. Not only are you the only children to be born to a female, but you are also the only twins to ever be born.

"My abilities are your abilities. I can control energy, matter, and the weather. There's so much more that has grown through the years, but it all started that way for me. You mean everything to me, and I couldn't let anything happen to you. If I'd stayed, they would have found me, killed your father, and taken you. I turned to Dorian for advice, especially since your father knew nothing about us."

Hadley noticed her sister glancing at her from time to time. She could feel the ice daggers shooting from Whitley's eyes. She had betrayed her by not telling her everything. She knew now by withholding information she thought made them different, she drove a deeper wedge between them.

"Okay, but get back to the part about dad telling you to leave," Whitley said with a hint of irritation in her voice. "We got the history lesson from Dorian."

"When I finally broke down and told him who I really am and that you girls were going to be special, he lost it. Looking back, I know he was just scared. We were in love. We had been together for years, and we had two beautiful little girls. We were a family. He looked at me like I was a stranger. He asked me to leave, and because I loved him so much, I did. I left, thinking he would calm down and think about it. I left thinking he would call me in a week or less, but he never called, and wouldn't answer when I finally called him."

Tahlia had to take a break to compose herself. After taking a few deep breaths and wiping the tears from her cheeks, she continued, "I tried to keep tabs on you guys. I tried to respect your father's wishes, but he clearly didn't want me in your lives. I did send you letters every week, so you would know I was thinking of you, and you were always the most important thing in my life. Clearly, your father didn't even want me to have that much contact with you."

Hadley wasn't sure what to think. Her father had always been such a great guy. He may have been focused on his career, but he had always taken care of them. It pained her to think he would keep their mother from them for all those years. Her mother had every reason to lie. She wanted them on her side. Hadley decided at that moment she wouldn't believe anything her mother said until she'd spoken with their father.

"Mom, if you don't mind, I think Whitley and I need some time alone to talk about everything," Hadley said gently.

Tahlia nodded and left the room, pausing briefly at the door to look at them both with reluctance all over her face.

It took a moment for Hadley to work up the courage to talk to her twin. She knew Whitley was beyond upset with her, but she had to talk to her about all this.

"Look, Whit, we need to talk."

"I agree." Whitley gave her a look that told her she was waiting for a decent explanation.

The Evolved

"First of all, I began to notice my abilities the first month we got our periods. I was crabby, and it literally felt like I had a rain cloud over my head all the time. I started watching carefully and began to draw connections between the freakish storms we had and the times I was angry or sad." Hadley paused and looked intently at her sister. "I should have told you, but I didn't because we have always shared everything. Physically, we're exactly alike. We think alike, talk alike, and share the same interests."

Whitley rolled her eyes. "You don't have to tell me about our life story. I was there."

Hadley took a deep breath and slowly let it out. "You're right. I just want you to understand. I thought this was something that would set us apart. I didn't want us to be different. We've always had each other."

"I get it. I'm not as mad about you discovering your abilities and not telling me. I've been thinking about it, and I think I may have done the same thing in your shoes. The part I'm angriest about is finding out you were looking for mom and didn't let me help you." Whitley was clearly stung.

"I started looking for mom on our sixteenth birthday. I remember our friends talking about their mother-daughter day—getting manicures and pedicures together. I felt a hot flash of anger inside because you and I never got to experience those things. We've always had each other, but I would have given anything for us to have a relationship with our mom." Hadley shrugged. "I didn't think you'd want to help. Every time I bring her up, you change the subject."

Whitley sighed. "You used to cry for her in your sleep."

"What?" Hadley was shocked. She'd been plagued with nightmares about her mother since she left.

"I used to lay awake at night listening to you crying. Sometimes I would sneak into bed with you and stroke your hair until you stopped. When you calmed down, I would either stay with you or sneak out and go back to my bed," Whitley whispered.

"I thought you ended up in my room because you were scared," Hadley said. "I didn't know. I'm sorry."

Whitley reached over and hugged her sister. "I love you, Hadley. You're my sister and my best friend. Nothing you do will ever change that. I wasn't happy to find out you were keeping things from me. It made me especially mad to find out from someone else. But I'm okay, I understand why you did it."

When she pulled away, Hadley smiled at her sister. "I'm glad we're okay. I was really worried you would be angry with me." Hadley and Whitley grinned at each other for a few moments.

"We really need to call dad. I think we need to hear his side of all this before we make any judgments about either of them. I don't want to hate mom, and I know you feel the same. But I also know we can't just take everything she said and forget the life we've had with dad." Whitley voiced the conflict Hadley was fighting inside.

Hadley nodded at her and pulled out her cell phone. Before she could press the speed dial, the phone started playing "Hail to the Chief."

The Evolved

Smiling at Whitley, she answered the phone and began the longest conversation of her life.

Chapter Nine:
Kerr

Kerr sat at the table in the formal dining room. He looked around at his new friends and smiled. He had always been a loner and never found himself surrounded by so many people filled with good intentions.

"Seems a little stupid to be eating pizza in such a fancy room," Thatcher said.

Nora laughed and smiled kindly at Thatcher. "This is the room we eat in. It's not supposed to be fancy, just tastefully decorated."

"Right, well, it's a lot nicer than any place I've ever lived," Thatcher responded quietly.

Dorian and Nora exchanged a look. Kerr knew Nora had been raised by Dorian, and he envied her chance to grow up knowing about their history. He hadn't really gotten a chance to talk to Nora yet. She was so quiet and smart. She had long, auburn hair that cascaded down her back in loose curls. Her green eyes crinkled as she smiled at him, and she had a wide beautiful smile that lit up her face. He felt like he shouldn't invade her privacy by reading her. Kerr didn't really understand, and he'd never experienced that before. He tried to clear his mind.

"So, Dorian, how long have you lived in Benton? I've never seen you around," Kerr asked.

"I've owned this home for thirteen years. We moved here when Nora started school. Tahlia and I posed as her aunt and uncle to enroll her. She was attending a private school over in Newall. As long as we paid them and she continued to exceed every expectation they had, they didn't care if we kidnapped her and kept her in a closet." Dorian laughed at his joke.

"Yikes, nothing like a creepy kidnapping scenario to put those of us who just met you at ease." Thatcher gave a short laugh and tried not to look nervous.

"How old are you now, Nora?" Kerr asked to change the subject.

"I just turned twenty. I graduated from college in May." Nora smiled shyly.

"Wow. I didn't finish my degree until I was twenty-three," Kerr said with surprise.

Nora blushed, and Kerr smiled at her, holding her gaze a moment longer than he intended. He looked away quickly, feeling the heat rise in his ears. He noticed the man they called Romulus smiling at him. He couldn't put his finger on it, but something about that man reminded him of his father. He nodded at Romulus and focused on his pizza.

"You know, you look just like my son," Romulus said.

"I was just thinking how much you look like my father." Kerr looked up.

"Well, that makes sense, considering I'm your many times' great-grandfather." Romulus smiled.

Kerr dropped his pizza and stared open-mouthed at Romulus. It was surreal to be sharing a pepperoni pizza with the man who essentially began his family tree.

"Don't look at me like that. You remind me of my wife. She always used to give me the most incredulous looks," Romulus said.

"Wife? Seriously loose term to describe an innocent young girl you ended up killing," Kerr snapped before he could stop himself.

He watched the darkness cloud over Romulus' face. He could feel the anger rolling off him. Kerr wasn't sure what was coming next, but he knew it wouldn't be good.

"You. Know. Nothing," he said through gritted teeth. Kerr could see the control he was fighting to keep. "I loved her. She was my everything."

Kerr sat in shocked silence as Romulus got up and strode out of the dining room. After a few moments, he heard a door slam.

"Romulus was right to leave," Dorian said beside him. "You shouldn't talk about things you can never understand." He slowly stood up and followed in his brothers' footsteps.

"Are you an idiot?" Nora spoke in a harsh tone.

"Um . . . " Kerr couldn't think of how to respond. Anything he said would sound like fourth-grade nonsense.

"That's what I thought. You don't even know him. How dare you judge the Old Immortals for their past. Especially the ones who cared too much about their future to allow their brothers to continue to marry and mate with human women." Nora looked at him with fire in her eyes. "He's right, you don't know anything. Romulus is the biggest teddy bear you will ever meet, and he wears his heart on his sleeve. He loved you before he even laid eyes on you."

Kerr could tell she was clearly disgusted with him, and that bothered him for some reason. He didn't know what made him say something so ugly. He looked around the table, trying to figure out what to do next. He was surprised to see tears streaming down Nora's face. He had definitely crossed a line.

Before he could say anything, Nora got up to leave but stopped when the phone began to ring. She turned to head into the kitchen, but her voice traveled back to Kerr and Thatcher at the table.

"Hello? . . . Oh, he's not available right now . . . I see . . . Well, I'm his granddaughter, could I help you? . . . In this kind of circumstance, I'm supposed to ask for a key phrase . . . And also with you . . . Okay, what do you need? . . . What? Are you sure? How can that be possible? . . . Where is he? . . . What is his name? . . . Thank you for the information, we will take care of this immediately." Kerr heard Nora hang up the phone and let out a low whistle.

He exchanged a look with Thatcher that told him they were both completely clueless. They waited for a few moments before realizing Nora would not be coming back to the dining room. Kerr stood and looked at Thatcher.

"Well, I don't know about you, but I want to find out what that was all about. Let's go, I'm sure if we wander around this place long enough, we'll find someone." Kerr motioned for Thatcher to follow him, and the two made their way back into the foyer.

Coming face to face with Tahlia, he saw the strain in her face and knew the time she spent with her daughters hadn't exactly gone the way she'd hoped. Kerr gave her a sympathetic shrug and filled her in on what they overheard from Nora's phone conversation.

"That seems odd. If she asked for the key phrase, it must be one of our scouts. I thought they were all on standby. We have all five of you," Tahlia said and turned down the hallway toward the library.

Thatcher and Kerr followed her and entered a room smelling of old paper. Kerr looked around, trying to avoid the eyes of the man he'd offended. Dorian and Romulus sat across from each other in oversized brown chairs. Romulus looked at Kerr with hurt in his eyes and quickly looked away.

Kerr didn't know what to do, so he walked up to Romulus and said the first thing that came to mind. "Look, I'm sorry I said what I did. All I know is the vague story Dorian told us. I shouldn't have been so quick to judge you."

Romulus nodded, looking directly into Kerr's eyes. Instantly, a flash filled his mind. Scenes from Romulus' life filled his head in rapid-fire. He saw the good

The Evolved

Romulus had done in his long life. He saw him watching over boys and men who all held a strong resemblance to them both. The final scene that flashed through his mind was the face of a beautiful woman with flowing black hair, dark brown eyes that were almost black, and a heart-shaped face. Her face was filled with love, joy, then pain, and anguish, and finally, her eyes were closed, her face a mask of death.

"Oh God," Kerr said. "I saw her. I just saw her, she was beautiful."

"I know. Her name was Anu," Romulus choked out. "You have her hair and my eyes. She died giving life to our son, Keiran. You could have been his twin."

A moment passed between them, and Kerr knew he had found the only man he would ever respect as much as his father.

The others had been quiet up until this moment, but Tahlia had to tell Dorian what Kerr and Thatcher overheard.

Romulus looked at Tahlia as though he didn't understand her. "Where is Nora? Did you see where she went?"

"No, she just left the kitchen and didn't say a word to us," Thatcher said.

"I'm here." Nora's voice rang out behind them.

When they turned and saw her dressed in comfortable traveling clothes and carrying a duffel bag, they knew something serious was going on.

"There is another. Brett, the scout, called to tell us he

discovered another Evolved. All the prophecies said there would be five, but somehow another of us has survived. His name is Malcolm." She still seemed to be in a state of shock.

"What prophecies?" Kerr asked, feeling out of the loop again.

"We can cover that later. Right now, we need to get to this Malcolm. Did he say whose he is?" Dorian asked with concern in his face.

"That's the worst part. He is descended from Absalom." Nora's face reflected the fear that rippled through the group.

"How did Absalom miss one? Where is he?" Tahlia asked with a strained voice.

"He's in Newall. We need to go now. We can't let him get to this one." Nora turned and headed down the hall. It only took a moment for everyone to jump to their feet and follow her.

Chapter Ten:
Whitley

Their father was not pleased. In fact, he decided to show his displeasure by hopping on his private jet and flying home. Whitley knew it would still be hours before he arrived, but her stomach was in knots at the thought of a family reunion.

"It will be okay, I promise. Dad will make a big deal out of this whole thing, but you know it's next to impossible to stuff a cat back in a bag without causing serious personal injuries." Hadley smiled wryly.

"But we are minors, he could forbid us to see mom. Even though she's been absent for most of our lives, I think this whole Evolved thing is going to make her a hot commodity in our lives now," Whitley responded.

Whitley took a deep breath and blew it out slowly. Their dad wasn't going to take this lightly, and she knew he would try to keep them from the new world they'd discovered. Whitley and Hadley knew they had to do everything in their power to get him to cooperate. The room had grown steadily warmer, and one glance at the vacant fireplace told Whitley the source of the temperature spike was sitting on the couch with her.

"Would you knock it off? I'm frying in here!" Whitley threw a pillow accusingly at her sister.

The Evolved

"Sorry, I'm just so nervous. Hold on." Hadley closed her eyes and attempted to meditate, but soon began giggling uncontrollably.

The girls fell into fits of giggles and were startled when the door to the den opened, and they found themselves face to face with the rest of the Evolved and Old Immortals.

Everyone stared at each other blankly for a few moments before Hadley and Whitley began giggling again, and it only got worse when Hadley laughed so hard she fell off the couch.

"Well, I can tell they're going to be useless on this mission." Nora rolled her eyes.

"Mission?" Whitley managed to say through the case of hiccups she'd developed.

"A scout called. They've found another Evolved. We need to get him before Silas finds him," Dorian said.

"Another Evolved? How?" Whitley asked.

Dorian shook his head and looked troubled.

"We need to figure something out fast. If our scout spotted this boy, it's only a matter of time before Absalom locates him," Tahlia said.

"I thought Absalom did the fire thing like me," Thatcher said.

"He does, but we all have many aspects to our abilities. Fire is his main ability, but he can also defy gravity. Remember, as he has also killed countless descendants of the Old Immortals, he has absorbed power. Because you and Malcolm are his last descendants, you share all his powers. Eventually, when we destroy him, his living descendants will inherit the abilities he has collected. Absalom has many abilities. We don't even know what all he is capable of, which is part of what makes him so dangerous. Silas has been his sidekick through it all, but Absalom has been careful to ensure he is less powerful and, therefore, submissive," Dorian answered.

"This guy is twisted," Thatcher said, shaking his head.

They discussed the plan and decided it would be less intimidating for Malcolm if only a few of them went. The small group would travel to the nearby town Newall to pick him up. They needed to be quick, but it was a sensitive mission.

Nora had already decided she was going, and she asked that Romulus and Whitley accompany her.

Whitley wasn't sure why she was asked to go along. She didn't even know how to control her power. What if she blew the kid up? She laughed in spite of the serious situation because this morning, her biggest worry had been whether or not to flirt with the coffee shop guy. It was funny how much life could change in only a few hours.

Once Nora and Romulus had everything they needed, Whitley followed them to the garage and got into a black Range Rover. Romulus was in the driver's seat, and Nora let Whitley sit shotgun. They drove in silence for a few minutes before Nora cleared her throat, indicating she had something to say.

The Evolved

"So, Whitley, how are you and Hadley feeling?" she asked carefully.

Whitley considered her answer carefully. "I think we're okay. It's a lot to take in, and I think it will be a long time before we're able to have even a semi-normal relationship with our mom."

"I know it's not really my place to say anything, but she really missed you. She's talked about you every day since I met her, and that was twelve years ago," Nora said.

"I believe it. We were so confused when mom left. We knew how much she loved us. We kept thinking we were in trouble and did something wrong to make her leave. Over the years, we learned to live without her. It's going to be an adjustment having two parents again." Whitley gave a small smile to Nora and Romulus.

Whitley wasn't sure what to make of Nora yet. She seemed sweet enough, but Whitley couldn't help but feel a sting of jealousy knowing that Nora had gotten to spend so many years with her mother. They drove in silence, and Whitley was left to think about the insane events of the day. Just this morning, her biggest problem was trying to figure out which shoes to wear with her outfit. Shaking her head, she turned to look out the window in time to see the sign welcoming them to Newall.

"He's thirteen. The scout said he usually hangs out at the skate park by Newall Central High School. He saw him there right before he called us." Nora's tone was all business.

Romulus pulled into a parking spot and turned off the Range Rover. He turned in his seat so he could see both Nora and Whitley.

"Now, this kid doesn't know what's coming. As far as we know, he hasn't even started to control his abilities. The only reason the scout recognized him as one of the Evolved is that he fell off his skateboard and scared himself when he realized he was hovering inches above the ground. His abilities indicate that he belongs to Absalom, so we need to hurry. It's only a matter of time before Absalom realizes he missed another one." Romulus studied them carefully, before continuing, "We need to be careful not to scare him off. He doesn't know it yet, but he needs our protection. Dorian did a good job of using the most basic of his abilities to draw you all to us, so we need to do our best not to send him running in the other direction."

Nora nodded, and Whitley contemplated what she'd just heard. Dorian drew them here? She thought back to a book she read about a girl who was in thrall to a warlock, and she wondered if they were all somehow in thrall to Dorian. Whitley shuddered and pushed the thought from her mind. She was drawn back to reality by the doors opening.

Whitley hopped out and followed Nora and Romulus up the slope that led them to the skate park. They stood together at the top of the hill and surveyed the area. In front of them was an open paved park with benches and trees spread throughout. All around the other edges were railings and stairs that gave the park a street appeal. A section to the left held a large oval bowl and two smaller, irregularly-shaped bowls. Whitley saw a group of boys going up and down a series of banks down the middle that led directly into a quarter pipe on either end.

Some commotion was coming from the other side of the park to the right. The small group exchanged glances and headed toward the disturbance. When they arrived, the half-pipe was surrounded by skaters of all ages. It was clear they were preparing themselves for a show. Romulus shot Nora a meaningful look, and she nodded her head in response. Whitley felt Romulus take her elbow and steer her a few feet away.

"I need you to focus because Nora is going to use her main ability now. You need to remember where you are and what you're looking at," Romulus whispered.

Whitley gave him a skeptical look but nodded her head. She looked at the crowd again. Nora had weaved her way into the middle and stood with her eyes closed. Suddenly, the crowd began to act confused. They looked around like they didn't know where they were. Whitley lost focus for a moment and caught a glimpse of the skate park in a rainstorm. She even felt the rain hitting her skin. Just as she reached up to see if her hair was wet, she felt Romulus grasp her arm again. She instantly saw the park as it had been before the rain, but the crowd had dispersed.

"What just happened?" she asked Romulus, unable to hide the shock in her voice.

"Nora can mess with your senses—make you see, feel, hear, taste things that aren't there," Romulus said with a smile. "Pretty cool, huh?"

Whitley was growing to like Romulus more every minute. He was like a big kid. After the crowd dispersed, only one person remained. He had been standing at the foot of the half-pipe and seemed to be the reason for the gathering crowd.

They came closer to the boy and found Nora already talking to him.

"Hi, you must be Malcolm," Nora said cheerily.

"Yeah. Who are you?" Malcolm asked warily.

"My name is Nora. I heard you could do some pretty neat tricks on that skateboard," Nora answered, then leaned in and said, "I can do some pretty neat tricks too."

"Really? Do you skateboard?" Malcolm rolled his eyes.

"Well, no. But if you close your eyes and concentrate, you'll find that it was never raining at all. I only made everyone think it was." Nora smiled.

Malcolm looked unsure but tried anyway. He was thirteen. Whitley knew from experience that thirteen-year-old boys were gullible and willing to try anything, no matter how stupid it made them look.

When Malcolm opened his eyes, he looked around with wide eyes. Whitley knew the approach Nora took probably just won them the only chance they had to get Malcolm to come along.

Chapter Eleven:
Malcolm

Malcolm stood in the skate park, watching the people who had just approached. He listened to what the girl, who called herself Nora, had to say. He knew she was telling the truth, but he had to pretend he was clueless.

Malcolm knew all about these people. His whole life had prepared him for this moment. He had to pretend to be the innocent boy they thought he was, otherwise, the whole plan would fall through.

He knew he would go with them. He'd always known he would. His Uncle Abe had been preparing him for this meeting for his whole life.

From listening to the conversation, he learned that the big guy was Romulus, and the other girl was Whitley. He knew who Romulus was from the stories he'd been told. He tried to pay attention to their conversation, but he was trying to figure out who Whitley was. She must be an Evolved, but she had to be one Absalom didn't know about. He knew all about Nora, Thatcher, and Kerr from the surveillance pictures Absalom's people had taken.

Malcolm heard them mention how to tell his parents he had to go with them. He had gone through life with his Uncle Abe, dragging him from town to town. His parents were dead. He knew how, he knew why, and most importantly, he knew who was responsible.

"Guys, it won't be hard to convince my uncle that I'm going off to camp or something. He doesn't know or care what I do most of the time," Malcolm said, pulling out his cell phone.

He sent a text to Uncle Abe and waited only a few minutes before he received a response that simply said, "K." Malcolm shrugged and told them it was okay for him to go.

Romulus looked troubled by the lack of concern his guardian showed him and exchanged a worried look with the girls. Everything was falling into place. Malcolm smiled sadly at them, then looked away, hoping he looked like a neglected child.

"Really, guys, it's no big deal. It's been like this forever," Malcolm said convincingly and was pleased when he saw them looking at him with pity.

Nora and Romulus led the way to their vehicle, leaving Whitley to hang behind and walk with him. She seemed nice, but he could tell she was uncomfortable.

"So, how old are you?" Whitley asked conversationally.

"Almost fourteen. My birthday is next week," he responded, trying to sound grown-up.

"I just found out about all this, too, so I know how you feel right now." Whitley patted him on the shoulder.

"Oh yeah, what's your superpower? Can you leap tall buildings in a single bound? Stop a train?" Malcolm said, only half-joking. He hadn't been told what abilities the others had.

Whitley smiled and took a few minutes to respond.

"You don't have to tell me, it's cool," he said, feeling frustration well up inside him.

"No, it's not that, I just don't really know how to explain it. I don't even know how to do it. My abilities started emerging this morning. I blew up all the lights in a book store," Whitley said, sounding confused.

"You can blow stuff up? That's way cooler than flying!" Malcolm felt himself getting excited about the other's abilities. Uncle Abe had told him how to obtain the abilities of others.

"Well, I don't really know if I can *blow stuff up*. I think I can mess with energy and matter. At least that's what Dorian and my mom told me. You'll meet them too," Whitley responded.

"Wicked! I don't really know what all this is. Do you think it's like superhero stuff?" Malcolm said, trying to sound like a normal thirteen-year-old.

Whitley laughed and told him she didn't think so. Under normal circumstances, Malcolm might have liked Whitley. She was pretty, and her round face broke into a wide smile easily. She was so new to the Evolved that maybe she wasn't like the others. Malcolm toyed with the idea of telling Whitley that she should go with him to help his uncle, but he already knew that was too big of a risk. Maybe she was playing dumb just like he was.

"So you just found out about this today, but you're

here picking me up? That has to be weird, right?" Malcolm asked, trying to get more information about her.

"Yes, actually. This morning my sister and I were just normal teenagers in a small town book store. Everything changed rather quickly, and so much has happened in the last eight hours that I'm still reeling," Whitley admitted.

"You have a sister?" Malcolm didn't think any of the Evolved had family left that could tie them to their ancestors. If Whitley had abilities, wouldn't her sister have them too?

"Mmhmm. My sister is back at the house. I guess she can do stuff to the weather. I haven't really gotten to see that yet, though," she replied.

"Cool. I don't have any siblings. My parents are dead, so my uncle is the only person I really know. Well, I have another uncle, too, but he isn't around as much. My aunt died a while ago, so he's been pretty upset," he said, hoping that didn't give too much away.

"I'm sorry to hear that. You must be pretty lonely. My father is away a lot on business, and our mother disappeared when we were little. We only just found out she was alive today," Whitley said wistfully.

Both her parents were alive. How was that possible? Did Absalom and Silas miss someone? If so, they were going to be pretty mad.

"So are your parents freak shows too?" Malcolm asked.

Before she could respond, there was a strange

vibration in the air. Malcolm felt the temperature drop and was struck with annoyance as he realized what it meant. He looked at Whitley and saw she felt it too. She reached over and took his hand and pulled him up the hill. They reached Romulus and Nora, who were standing in tense positions. They could feel it, and they didn't look happy.

"We need to get out of here now," Nora said quietly.

"Get them in the car. I will try to keep them busy while you get back to Dorian. There's no way we can fight without one of them getting hurt." Romulus was pointing at Whitley and Malcolm.

Nora shook her head. "Either we all go together, or I stay behind. I can hide and keep them from seeing you as you get them back home. That way, if something happens and they catch up to you, they'll have your protection."

Malcolm watched as Nora and Romulus exchanged a look and embraced. When they pulled away, Nora wiped tears from her face. She took a step forward as though she wanted to hug Whitley too, but stopped herself, nodded at both of them, and took off at a sprint.

"Get in."

Malcolm and Whitley saw Romulus holding open the back door of the Range Rover.

"And stay low."

Malcolm obeyed immediately, knowing this was the final step in his infiltration, but Whitley stayed back.

The Evolved

"Why is Nora staying?" she challenged Romulus.

"She has to. Silas and Absalom are almost here. Now get in the car," Romulus said through gritted teeth.

Whitley shook her head and stood her ground.

"Whitley, come on!" Romulus yelled, making the strain in his voice obvious.

"I am not leaving Nora. She needs help. You need to take Malcolm and go. If he belongs to Absalom, he will be the target. I don't think they'll hurt me without Hadley here, they want us both." Whitley was all business but stopped to give Romulus a pleading look. "Please, Romulus. My mom has raised Nora like another daughter. I know that if anything happened to her, I would never forgive myself for the pain it will cause her."

Romulus dropped his head and shoulders in defeat. "You are more like your mother than you will ever know," he said with a fierce pride in his voice.

He placed a hand on Whitley's shoulder and kissed the top of her head. She ran after Nora. Romulus hopped in, and soon they were pealing out of town.

Chapter Twelve:
Nora

Nora tucked herself into an alley behind a dumpster. She could feel them coming, and they were close. She could only hope she would be able to buy Romulus enough time to get the others to safety.

She stiffened, hearing approaching footsteps. She focused on an image of an empty alley and projected it to anyone who may be coming. Sitting quietly against a brick building, she waited for the intruder to move on.

"Nora?" A voice whispered, breaking her concentration. It was Whitley.

Nora stood up and peeked around the corner of the dumpster. She saw relief flood Whitley's face and felt a grin creep onto her own.

"What are you doing here? I saw the Rover drive away," she asked.

"I couldn't leave you here alone. I mean, I'm basically your sister," Whitley responded.

Nora felt her face flush and rushed to hug Whitley. "You have no idea what this means to me. But I don't want you to get hurt. You don't know how to control your ability."

The Evolved

"Don't worry about me, maybe I'll accidentally do something brilliant." Whitley smiled.

The moment passed quickly as the temperature fluctuated again. She exchanged a nervous look with Whitley, then grabbed her hand and led her to the mouth of the alley.

"Silas likes to use his favorite ability—ice. He can make everything freeze, even in the middle of the summer. Absalom can set fire to anything, even if it's fireproof. I actually think it's a bit funny when he and Absalom are together. It's like they're having a tug of war with the temperature," Nora said quietly.

"Imagine what would happen if they ran into Hadley," Whitley answered.

Nora nodded with wide eyes. She hadn't thought about that dynamic. It was more evident than ever that they could not get their hands on the twins. If they absorbed their powers, Absalom and Silas would be unstoppable.

Nora looked out at the park that was busy again, now that the effects of her ability had worn off. She frowned and closed her eyes. She could feel them, they were close. Her eyes snapped open and instantly focused on two figures loping toward them.

"Listen, you need to really focus. I know you haven't been able to control yourself yet, but if you're going to figure it out, now would be perfect," she whispered urgently to Whitley.

Whitley nodded and closed her eyes. Nora grinned as she took a step out of the alley. "This is gonna be fun."

All at once, the Old Immortals recognized her. She could see the change in their bodies as they continued forward. Nora could almost imagine the wicked smiles on their faces. They were confident, and they were sure they would be gaining more power today.

A chill ran down her spine, and she felt her hair stand on end. Something was happening. Nora chanced a glance at Whitley and relished the look of triumph on her face. She would not be alone in this fight.

"Ah, little Nora Lowell. You've grown since we last met," Silas sneered.

"I've grown in more than one way, Silas," Nora spat out his name.

"All the power I feel can't be from you. Have you found an Evolved playmate?" Silas asked playfully.

"Yes, she has." Whitley stepped forward.

Nora felt Whitley come to stand beside her. Energy was crackling in the air. Whitley was a quick study.

"Oh, who is this?" Absalom asked. "No, don't tell me. How is this even possible?"

Nora cringed as the Old Immortals exchanged excited glances. Whitley looked so much like her mother that it was not difficult to determine whose child she was. She knew they would now be focused on Whitley, and it would only be a matter of time before they got a matching set. She had to get Whitley out of here before they got too many ideas.

"I'm going to make you invisible," Nora whispered to Whitley.

The Evolved

"You can do that?" Whitley asked, shocked.

"Well, kind of. I mean, I can make it so they can't see you. They're looking at you like a piece of meat," Nora responded disgustedly.

Nora smiled as Whitley melted from view.

"What's this? You can make things disappear now?" Silas asked incredulously, his nostrils flaring in his long, narrow nose.

"Don't be a fool. She's just messing with our heads. The girl isn't gone, she's still here somewhere." Absalom looked around.

"Oh, she's here somewhere. But you'll have to kill me in order to find her. Think you can manage that?" Nora was feeling cocky.

"Well, I've been itching to kill someone today," said Silas with venom in his voice.

Absalom shifted and began to form a ball of fire in his hands. Before he could do anything with it, electricity crackled in the air as Whitley shot past her. Nora could see her, but they couldn't, and that girl had moves. The impact she made when she collided with Absalom was intense. Nora saw his body ripple as Whitley shot straight through him. Absalom was shocked and gasping for breath.

"This girl has inherited her mother's abilities. I have to say, I am so intrigued by her mere existence. None of the other Old Immortal females could have children. Why her mother?" Silas mused.

Nora began to feel her nerves creeping up on her.

Something wasn't right. They hadn't mentioned Malcolm at all. Their focus had completely changed the second they saw Whitley. Nora hadn't planned on having to defend someone. This was just supposed to be a distraction. She had to do something.

"Well, this visit has been so nice, but I think we should be going," Nora said awkwardly, searching for her next move. Then it hit her. "Oh, I almost forgot, I was so sorry to hear about what happened with Thatcher." Nora knew her reference to the death of Caprice would rattle his cage and end the meaningless banter.

Silas looked confused as a look that resembled loss crossed his face.

"I should clarify. I meant I was sorry he didn't kill you too," Nora said sweetly.

Silas snarled and threw out his arms. A burst of power came from him, and the ground began to shake as the temperature plummeted. Ice shot up around them in a circle, and people began to scream. Whitley grabbed Nora's hand, and she squeezed in response. Nora began to panic. What was she thinking of going up against these two? Especially in such a public place. The humans around them would be killed if Silas unleashed another earthquake.

Her heart began to beat quickly, and she felt faint. This hadn't happened before. Maybe she was just nervous. The world spun around her, and confusion sank in. Nora closed her eyes to keep herself from throwing up.

"Well, that was new." Dorian's voice broke through the waves of nausea.

The Evolved

Nora opened her eyes and found herself standing in the library at her house, still holding Whitley's hand. Silas and Absalom were nowhere in sight. Somehow, she had transported Whitley and herself to the safest place she knew.

Chapter Thirteen:
Dorian

Dorian smiled to himself as he looked at Nora. He knew she was slowly growing more powerful, inheriting the abilities he had enjoyed in his youth. It seemed the death of Caprice had set the prophecies in motion, and the Evolved were growing at an accelerated pace.

"How did I do that?" Nora looked pale as she sank to the floor. "Where are Silas and Absalom?"

"Nora, your ability is growing," Dorian said gently. "I'm inclined to believe you're all going to see a burst in power now that you're all together. The prophecies will start soon."

Dorian felt a confusion settle over the room, and he looked at the faces he'd seen grow from a distance. He'd been waiting for them to grow more comfortable with the idea of having powerful abilities. The discovery of Malcolm was troubling. There had only been five Evolved in the prophecies. He wasn't sure where Malcolm fit in, but he knew his appearance wasn't going to bode well for one of the Evolved.

He listened to Nora and Whitley share their story about their encounter with Silas and Absalom. He was concerned about the interest they showed in Whitley but knew it was expected. The only positive was that they still didn't know there were two of them. He needed to keep it that way for as long as possible. If they never saw them together until the inevitable battle, it could give them the element of surprise they needed to win.

"They really didn't mention the boy at all?" Dorian asked Nora.

"No. It was strange. They didn't even seem distracted, and they seemed more interested in witty banter than anything else," Nora said.

"Well, Absalom always did like to play with his food," Tahlia said.

"Yuck!" Hadley and Whitley said in unison.

"He really eats people? That's not an ability I'm going to inherit, right?" Thatcher said in shock.

Dorian and Tahlia laughed. "No, he doesn't really eat people, I was being facetious."

"Oh good," Thatcher said, not completely convinced.

"Absalom killed my father," Kerr said suddenly.

Dorian looked at Kerr. He'd been quiet since the girls returned. He should have known Kerr would see everything they saw within a few moments. Dorian was kicking himself for not realizing that Kerr wouldn't know which of the Old Immortals was responsible for the death of Cole Mason.

"Yes, he did," Dorian said simply.

"I can still see him. I see him every time I think about

my father. Every memory of my father is haunted by his face," Kerr said in a strained voice.

Before anyone could say anything to him, the library door opened, and Romulus walked in with Malcolm. Romulus looked at Nora and Whitley with interest, before introducing Malcolm to the rest of the Evolved.

Taking a deep breath, he decided now was as good a time as any to explain what would be coming next. So far, all he'd told them was a history lesson, but they had no idea what the future held, and it was his job to tell them.

"Romulus, Tahlia, I think it is time to share the rest of the story with the Evolved."

Romulus nodded, and Tahlia took a seat.

"When the Old Immortals discovered their power was being dispersed amongst their descendants, they began to worry about their future. The Creator saw this and felt sorrow because, through the years, we had never questioned or worried about what our Creator had in store for us. The Creator appeared to three of our number in dreams. The first had an unwavering faith in the Creator's ability to guide our paths, the second possessed a hope for the future, no matter what it meant for the Old Immortals, and the third had experienced and demonstrated great love in all that he did." Dorian paused to allow questions but found there were none.

"In their dreams, they were each told to journey to the sacred meeting place where the Old Immortals worshiped the Creator. When they arrived at the temple, they saw the bright white light the Creator often chooses to appear as. The three became known as the Virtues." Dorian paused to allow himself a sip of water.

"The Virtues returned with the Book of Prophecy. The Creator had given them a glimpse into what the future held for our kind and our descendants. The prophecies told us enough to know how important the future would be and where we would be at this moment."

Dorian could see his words sinking into the Evolved. Hadley and Whitley were holding hands, staring at the fire, both biting their lower lip. Thatcher was concentrating on the floor with a furrowed brow while Malcolm looked confused and terrified. Kerr was pacing.

"You were the three. You are the Virtues," Kerr said with absolute certainty.

Romulus stepped forward and put a hand on Kerr's shoulder. "Yes, son, we are. And we are all that remains of the Old Immortals who chose to follow the Creator's plan."

They looked at each other for a moment, then Kerr nodded, and resigned himself to the couch.

"Dorian has the most faith I've ever seen in one being," Tahlia said, revealing the first of the Virtues.

"And Tahlia has more hope than all of us put together." Romulus beamed at his sister with pride.

"So that leaves love. It makes sense to me that you would represent love after seeing the glimpses of your life." Kerr smiled at Romulus.

Dorian was pleased to see Kerr and Romulus sharing so much already. He knew how important Kerr was to his brother. He felt Romulus had suffered enough through the years of watching and waiting.

"Okay, so what did this creator tell you three?" Thatcher asked. "Can you skip the big show and just tell us? I'm getting pretty tired."

Dorian smiled kindly. It would take time for Thatcher to warm up to them.

He continued, "Well, the Creator was trying to show us the reason we were here. After all the years of allowing us to help the human race, he was finally ready to show us his master plan. We were created to usher in the New Era. The Era led by our descendants. We were the tools the Creator used to bring forth the future he had in mind for his world."

Nora had regained her equilibrium and felt it was her turn to share. Over the years, she studied their history and had come to know it as well as the Virtues themselves.

"The Creator has always wanted to bring the human race full circle. In the beginning, the Creator was able to walk with humans—teach them, and lead them. But through the years, humans lost that connection. Because of their attitudes and actions, they were forced to live in ignorance. Some of the humans continued to be humbled by the one who had created them, while others felt he had abandoned them and decided to raise their families without the knowledge, love, and guidance of the Creator."

The Evolved

"Whoa, this is starting to sound like some kind of crazy cult," Thatcher said with his hands raised defensively in front of him. "I mean, I've met a lot of religious fanatics in my life who all think they're right. I am not interested in some weird religious stuff."

Dorian, Nora, Romulus, and Tahlia laughed loudly.

"I don't think you quite understand, Thatcher. This isn't a cult, and unfortunately, your *membership* isn't really negotiable, it's just who you are. The Creator is the inspiration for every god that has ever been. No matter what religious preference a person may have, no matter what various deities they think they're worshiping, they are all the same one. The Creator has many names. He has many homes, many languages, and many aspects." Romulus smiled broadly.

For a moment, there was complete silence as the concept of every god being the only one settled in. Dorian waited patiently for the questions he was sure would come, but the first one was not what he had expected.

"So, what you're saying is that all those times in history when people killed each other over their religion, it was pointless? All those people died for nothing," Malcolm said quietly.

Dorian tried to decide how best to explain. "Yes, Malcolm, that is exactly what we're saying. It is unfortunate, but it has happened time and time again. And unfortunately, the world isn't going to magically accept the New Era you will be responsible for. More will die pointlessly, of that I have no doubt."

"Wait a minute, the gods of every religion are different. They punish in different ways, they demand different forms of worship from their followers, and they all have their own set of wrong and right." Whitley began to argue.

"Ah, there it is," Dorian said. "You're not talking about the Creator. You're talking about religion. Belonging to a certain religion and belonging to the Creator are two different things. If you possess faith in your Creator, hope in the future your Creator has in store for you, and demonstrate the love your Creator instilled in you, you are following the right path, no matter what any religion has twisted those things to be."

"So, tell us about the prophecies. How many are there? Do they mention us by name?" Hadley wondered, perched on the edge of her seat.

"Well, there are six. They don't mention you by name. There is one referring to the arrival of the Evolved, there is one referring to who the Evolved will be, and we have come to understand which individual prophecy is about each of you. We haven't been able to figure out where you fit in, though, Malcolm. I guess you are proof that the Creator can change his plans at any given moment," Dorian said, trying to hide the strain of worry in his voice.

"I think we should give you each your prophecy in private, but we can start with the first because it involves all of us." Tahlia smiled.

Romulus stepped forward and took a deep breath. "The Evolved will be drawn together in the month of the great harvest. They will join the Virtues in ending the Present Era. All that has passed before will be known to them, and all that is to come will depend on them."

Silence filled the library. Dorian looked at each of the Evolved. He knew this would be a lot to ask of them, and he knew they would be apprehensive of what was to come, but he also knew there was no escaping one's destiny.

Chapter Fourteen:
Thatcher

As he lay on the bed in the room he'd been told was his, he couldn't help reliving the events of the day. Thatcher had heard enough. This was overwhelming. It wasn't as though he asked to take part in all this. If they needed an extra spot for the kid, they could give his prophecy to Malcolm. These thoughts kept spinning around in his mind, but he couldn't bring himself to voice his opinion out loud.

As crazy as all this sounded, it made sense to him. He had never belonged anywhere, but from the moment he met Dorian and the others, he felt at home. Thatcher had always longed to find people who accepted him as he was; people he didn't feel the need to hide his ability from. And finally, here he was, in a whole house full of freaks like him.

So why the doubt? Why was he rebelling so much against everything he had ever wanted? Taking a deep breath, he rolled over and buried his face in the pillow. As soon as he was face down, he let out a scream of frustration.

He knew why he was feeling so doubtful, but he didn't want to admit it to himself. After everything he had done in his life, everyone he had hurt, and the times he could have moved on but allowed himself to continue to wallow in self-pity, he didn't think he deserved this. Thatcher would not let himself believe he deserved to feel welcome, loved, or wanted.

At that moment, he did something he had never allowed himself to do; he let go. He opened the flood gates of his life and sobbed uncontrollably into the pillow.

Thatcher allowed himself to fully relive the events he had blocked out his whole life. He released all the pain, frustration, anger, and emptiness he'd carried with him from the day his parents died. He didn't know how long he lay there. His body racked with sobs long after he ran out of tears to shed.

Thatcher woke to find himself sprawled across his bed. For the first time in his life, he hadn't had any nightmares. He rolled over to find Steggie perched on the nightstand. Thatcher had never slept without him. He began to stretch but froze in place. There was something different in the air. Thatcher sat up and cautiously glanced around the room. He was alone. He listened carefully, but there was nothing to hear. He got up and checked the closet. His duffel bag was inside, but nothing else.

He turned on the small lamp on the nightstand, bringing a dull glow to the large bedroom. The room had been painted gray on three walls, and the fourth wall had a zig-zag pattern of grey, green, and navy blue. The bedding had the same design as the wall. When Dorian showed him to this room earlier, he felt like the room had been intended for him all along. There was a television mounted above the dresser, which was next to the bathroom door. There were a few gaming magazines on the nightstand and a top-of-the-line video game system on the dresser. He could get used to this.

He tried to thumb through one of the magazines, but still couldn't shake the feeling that something was going on, so he decided to peer into the hallway. Thatcher slowly opened the door. In the hallway, he realized his fellow freaks were also anxiously poking their heads out of their doors and staring down the hall.

"What's going on?" he chanced a whisper to his nearest neighbor, Kerr.

"I'm not sure. I woke a few minutes ago and just felt strange. I thought I heard someone call my name," Kerr replied with a strained voice.

The group cautiously came out of their rooms and met in the center of the hallway. Thatcher looked at each of them in turn and realized Malcolm was missing. Maybe he was the one calling to him? The foursome wordlessly decided to investigate together and walked as quietly as possible along the wall to the balcony overlooking the foyer. When they came to the top of the staircase, they could see nothing amiss. Directly across from them, they could see the black abyss of hallway containing the rooms of Nora and the three Old Immortals.

"It doesn't look like anyone else is up. Maybe we all heard a noise," whispered Hadley.

"No, it was overwhelmingly silent when I thought I heard someone call my name. I was awake, reading one of the books on the bookshelf in my room," Kerr responded.

Thatcher looked at each of them in turn and realized they were just as confused as he was.

Kerr led the way as they headed downstairs, with Whitley following closely behind. Thatcher turned around to check on Hadley and found her face strained with worry. He hadn't had much time to talk to either of the twins. When Whitley left with Romulus and Nora, everyone sat in the library waiting for them to return. Thatcher had helped Hadley clean up after dinner, but they hadn't really spoken much. She mostly asked questions about the time he spent on the run after his encounter with Silas, the psycho.

"What's wrong, Hadley?" he whispered quietly.

"I'm worried about Malcolm. Do you think he's still in his room?" asked Hadley.

Kerr and Whitley had disappeared into the darkness below, and Thatcher didn't want to chance making a lot of noise calling out for them if there was someone in the house looking to harm them.

"We need to go look for him," Thatcher said simply.

Hadley nodded her agreement and reached out her hand for him to take. He gave her a look that must have read *yeah right* because she gave him a look that clearly read *stop being such a boy*. They went back down the hallway they came from to check his room.

When they walked into his bedroom, it was clear he was an unexpected guest. Unlike every other room he had been in, this room felt clean and empty. The walls were cream, and the décor was simplistic, but well put together. This had clearly been a guest room rather than a room thoughtfully prepared for one of the Evolved. It made Thatcher a little sad, considering how accustomed he had become to being an unwelcome misfit. He wondered if Malcolm was feeling like an outcast.

"This is absurd. Where could he have gone?" Hadley said as she looked in his closet and under the bed.

"Do you think he went down the hall to see one of the Old Immortals?" Thatcher asked.

"Maybe. I can't believe we didn't notice he was missing," Hadley replied.

Thatcher shrugged and offered her his hand as they headed back out in the hall. It felt strange holding someone's hand. He hadn't let anyone this close in years. He grinned to himself. It felt strange, but it felt good.

Once they'd checked every room in their wing, they took the stairway down into the darkness to find Whitley and Kerr.

Thatcher couldn't help but smile when Hadley squeezed his hand. He squeezed back in reassurance and led her toward the kitchen. As they came around the island, they could see the hallway that led to the library. The library door stood slightly ajar, and there was a beam of light pouring out of it.

"Well, here goes nothing," Thatcher said and pulled on Hadley to lead her to the library.

The Evolved

But Hadley wouldn't budge.

Thatcher turned to see her staring open-mouthed out the window. He leaned closer to get the same view she had and couldn't believe what he saw. Malcolm was outside, talking to someone who looked like he could have been his brother. The cold feeling of dread he felt wash over him told him exactly who this was.

Absalom.

Thatcher pulled Hadley down to the floor. "That guy has to be Absalom. I can feel it. What is he doing here, and why is he talking to Malcolm? Could that little brat be a spy?"

Hadley grabbed his face in her hands. "Pull it together, Thatcher. We don't know what's going on. We don't even know what kind of powers he has. Maybe he can do some kind of mind control or something."

Thatcher's face felt hot under Hadley's touch; he nodded slowly and cleared his throat. But Hadley held eye contact with him. He watched her beautiful face as something seemed to cross her mind. He hadn't noticed how long her eyelashes were before, or the little freckle she had right below her right eye. Unconsciously, he reached up and touched it with his forefinger. She grinned and dropped her hands from his face. In the pale light from the moon, he could see she was embarrassed. And he couldn't deny feeling the same.

"You have beautiful eyes," Thatcher said.

Hadley smiled and looked away.

The moment passed and left Thatcher feeling exhilarated and confused. He didn't really know what had passed between them, but when she took his hand again, it felt different than it had moments before.

Chapter Fifteen:
Kerr

Whitley sat next to him on the couch. They had made their way through the halls to the open door of the library. They were surprised to find Dorian sitting in the center of the room in the lotus position. Nora was in the corner, curled up in an oversized chair.

"I'm so glad you heard me calling," Dorian said quietly.

Kerr and Whitley exchanged confused looks.

Dorian continued to meditate in silence. Kerr looked up and saw Nora give him a shrug and a reassuring smile. Kerr sat on the edge of the couch, listening intently for the others. When he and Whitley got downstairs, they rounded the stairs into the living room. He thought he heard someone moving in the darkness, but Whitley pulled his arm and led him to the library.

He wasn't sure where the others had ended up, but he knew they would hear Dorian calling to them. Nora got up and came over to them, smiling warmly.

"I've been waiting for you guys. They're going to share the prophecies with us now. Dorian said he feels that something is off, and the sooner we all know what is to come, the sooner we will be prepared to face it." She laughed lightly. "I've been waiting for this for a very long time! The prophecies are the only part of our history they haven't taught me about."

Kerr hadn't thought much about how different this was for Nora. She was used to the abilities, she was used to the strange history they all shared, and she was the only one who was raised in a safe and happy environment. The sadness and jealousy he felt thinking about how much he'd missed out on were much more intense than any he had experienced in his life thus far.

"You are so lucky," he blurted out.

Nora gave him a hurt and confused look. "So are you."

Kerr was about to ask what she meant by that when the library door opened, and Thatcher came in, followed closely by Hadley.

Thatcher's eyebrows were knit together in concern, and Hadley looked a little panicked. Kerr was on his feet in an instant. He had already seen it.

"Are you sure it was him?" Kerr asked Thatcher, catching him off guard.

"No, I'm not. But it was strange. I felt a connection. Like a thread was strung between us," he answered.

"What's going on?" Dorian asked.

The library door opened one more time, and Romulus entered, followed closely by Tahlia. They wore the same look of panic that was still etched on the faces of the other two Evolved. It was clear Absalom had, in fact, made an appearance.

"It's the boy, Dorian. Malcolm. He was with him. Absalom has returned," Romulus said with a mixture of sorrow and shock.

Whitley and Nora were huddled together near the couch, looking at them all in terror. After their encounter earlier, it was no surprise they were so tense.

Dorian looked at them all. He seemed to be processing the situation.

"We need to leave," he said simply.

"What about Malcolm?" Thatcher asked in disbelief. "What if Absalom is controlling him? I mean, the kid kept talking about growing up with his uncle, right? How could he even know Absalom?"

Dorian looked at Thatcher sadly. "No one wants to believe that more than I do. But something is wrong. This boy suddenly appears out of nowhere when all the Evolved are finally under one roof, so we did what we would be expected to do. We went and got him, and who showed up? I'm sorry, Thatcher, but I feel this was a trap. It's the only explanation for Malcolm not being part of the Creator's plan. "

"Plans change! Who says any of us are going to follow any of these prophecies you keep talking about? I don't have to do anything I don't want to. Maybe Absalom outsmarted this Creator you're so fond of," Thatcher shouted angrily.

Dorian stood quietly, just staring at Thatcher. Kerr watched the exchange, feeling the anguish pouring from them both. At that moment, Kerr wished there was a way for him to make them see they wanted the same thing and felt the same way.

"You can," Romulus whispered in his ear. "But it is not up to us to solve the problems of the world. Life would improve exponentially if we could just intervene and solve it all. But we cannot. They must choose."

Kerr only understood part of his point. "They must choose." What were they supposed to choose? He had to trust that Romulus knew what he was talking about, so he simply nodded.

Dorian and Thatcher were still having a staring contest in the middle of the room. He noticed the room seemed to be divided. Behind Dorian, Whitley and Nora stood together, next to Kerr and Romulus. Hadley and Tahlia stood closer to Thatcher, as though they were swayed by his argument. He realized Tahlia only stood where she did because of Hadley, and Hadley was staring intently at Thatcher.

"Thatcher, you have to come with us." Hadley was clearly distressed. "I saw him too. I know he's just a kid, but he may not know any better."

Kerr looked at the others. Whitley was concentrating on her sister's face, Romulus had a hand on Nora's shoulder, Tahlia had taken Hadley's hand, and Nora seemed to be thinking hard. In fact, Nora looked ill, and Kerr began to feel it too. He looked up and discovered the room was getting blurry. He didn't know what was happening, but he instinctively took hold of Nora with one hand and grabbed Whitley's arm with the other. The sick feeling got so intense, he closed his eyes tightly until it suddenly stopped.

He opened his eyes. Not only were they no longer in the library, but they were also no longer indoors. They were at the top of a mountain in the middle of nowhere.

"It's been a long time, hasn't it, brother?" Romulus smiled broadly at Dorian, who was staring around in disbelief.

"It seemed a fitting place to present the prophecies. I can't believe I did that," Nora said weakly as she leaned on Romulus for support.

Kerr looked around him. They stood in the ruins of a small building. It seemed oddly familiar to him, but he had never been in any such place. It was beautiful. The trees parted perfectly to allow the early morning sun to shine through.

"Where are we? What did you do?" demanded Thatcher.

"We are where it all began," Tahlia whispered.

Realization dawned in the quiet morning light. No wonder this place seemed so familiar, he had seen it in the glimpses he'd had of Romulus' life. The years hadn't been kind, and all that was left of the temple was a circle of pillars of varying heights. It had once been magnificent. Kerr looked around and saw what must have been the faded memory of what this place had been. He could see the pillars standing tall and the table in the middle of the open temple. He saw where the Virtues sat when they came to this sacred place. He realized he was experiencing a connection with a place rather than a person; he saw what this place had seen, rather than living through the

The Evolved

memories of another human mind. Kerr knew he should feel a sense of shock at this recent development, but a few moments ago he was standing in a library thousands of miles away. Nothing surprised him now.

Kerr took a seat on one of the pillars and watched as the others followed suit. Romulus came forward and handed Dorian a well-worn book. Dorian nodded, gazing at the pages in what could only be described as longing. The enormity of it all came crashing down on Kerr as he watched the Virtues take their places around what remained of the stone table. They had spent centuries waiting for this moment, and they had devoted their entire existence to preserving these books for this group of misfits. They'd watched their family die off one by one and knew that was the way it was supposed to be. Kerr realized he'd seen all of this through the eyes of Romulus, and while the loss and sadness were overwhelming, he felt the fierce love flowing through him and knew that none of the journey would be forgotten. But the journey was never important. He looked up at Romulus and saw the tears shining in his eyes. He was ready for this.

"We will start with the group prophecy," Tahlia said.

The group waited with bated breath for the prophecy that could change their lives.

Dorian took a deep breath and began, "Five will remain. The orphan, the divided, the heart, and the brave. They will be the final hope of mankind, and through them, all life will change."

Kerr let the words soak into him and thought about

what they could mean. He thought the prophecy would be more specific, and he thought it would tell them what was expected of the Evolved.

The feelings were swirling around. He could feel the confusion emanating from his fellow Evolved. He didn't know who was who in the prophecy, and he didn't know what it meant. He looked at the now-familiar faces around him. Were they the final hope of mankind?

"We have identified your individual prophecies based on the descriptions of the five remaining ancestors. Would you like to receive these prophecies alone or together?" Romulus asked.

"Together," they said as one. In any other situation, they would have found the moment amusing, but they each wore a mask of seriousness.

"Thatcher, please stand and receive your prophecy," Dorian announced.

Kerr watched Thatcher go forward to receive his prophecy and felt his stomach begin to flutter nervously.

Dorian smiled kindly at Thatcher as he stood before the Virtues. "Thatcher, you are the orphan. You are the only Evolved who came from two descendants of the Old Immortals. You have never found a home you could belong in because you always belonged to us. Are you ready to receive your prophecy?"

Thatcher's face was full of more questions than answers, but he still managed to nod his head.

The Evolved

"Your heart and mind are at odds. You must learn to accept the differences and choose the path that honors both. Do not be led astray by the appearance of innocence." Dorian motioned for Thatcher to take his seat, which he did with a look of concentration.

Kerr watched as Hadley and Whitley were summoned forth.

"Hadley and Whitley, you are the divided. As identical twins, you are made from one that is divided in two," Tahlia explained their title with tears in her eyes. "Are you ready to receive your prophecy?"

"We are," they said together.

"Although you are the same, you may go in different directions. But your greatest strengths appear when you are as one." Tahlia stepped forward and kissed both girls on the cheek before they sat back down.

Nora was called forth next. Dorian grinned proudly at her as she stood in front of him with her head held high.

"Nora, you are the heart. Your compassion for others has always been your greatest strength. Are you ready to receive your prophecy?" Dorian smiled widely at her.

"Yes, I am," Nora whispered.

"You may think you are the end, but the beginning will come from within you," Dorian finished with a raw edge to his voice.

Kerr felt his nerves building as Nora slowly took her seat and began staring at her hands. Kerr had a million questions rolling around in his head. He was at a loss to decipher the prophecies his friends had received. He heard Romulus call his name, and the world spun as he came forward on wobbly legs.

"Kerr, you are the brave. You have learned to trust your ability to help you through any situation. Your bravery has led you through situations most people would turn from. Are you ready to receive your prophecy?"

"I am," Kerr answered with a voice that held none of the nerves he'd felt moments before.

"You know what has been, and sense what is to come. But you must open your heart to the present, or the future will not be," Romulus finished with a hopeful look directed at Kerr.

He went over and took his seat between Whitley and Thatcher. The tension was mixed with confusion as the prophecies sank into their heads.

Chapter Sixteen:
Malcolm

"What do you want me to do now?" Malcolm asked Absalom.

"I need you to win Thatcher over. He possesses the rest of the power that you should have. As long as he lives, you will never claim all of your abilities. Once you win him over, bring him to me," Absalom said.

Malcolm nodded. "So once I bring him to you, what will happen to him?"

"That is none of your concern. Don't forget your place in all this, boy," Absalom snarled.

"You're going to kill him, aren't you?" he asked quietly.

"No. I will not kill him," Absalom answered.

"You won't?" Malcolm felt a surge of hope. He had taken a liking to Thatcher. They were basically brothers, after all.

"No, that will fall to you. You will kill him to absorb his power. You will blame his death on me when you rejoin the Evolved and take your place in the New Era. They will accept you, and you will carry my legacy," Absalom replied with only a hint of the evil he held inside him.

The Evolved

Malcolm left Absalom and made his way back into the house. He knew what was required of him and planned to pull it off. He'd been raised by Uncle Abe since before he could remember. His parents were both dead. He didn't know what happened, and he didn't care. All he knew was that it all had to do with The Evolved.

In order for them to fulfill the prophecies, they had to be the only remaining descendants of the Old Immortals. Abe had saved him. Malcolm had survived to prove that the future wasn't set in stone.

He remembered the day his Uncle Abe revealed himself as Absalom, one of the last remaining Old Immortals. Abe told Malcolm that he should be dead. He told him that his parents died because the Creator had chosen the five he would use to bring about his plans. What gave the Creator the right to decide who would live and who would die? Absalom trained him and showed him how to use his abilities. He taught him about the past and prepared him for the future.

The day the scout saw him in the park was planned. Where he would be when the Evolved came for him was planned. Absalom and Silas had set everything up. He knew they wouldn't be far behind when he was picked up, but he hadn't expected Absalom to follow him here.

He realized rather quickly that, while the plan was still to get rid of Thatcher, Absalom had his eyes on a new prize. Apparently, Whitley and her twin Hadley were some special limited-edition set because Abe was practically foaming at the mouth when he told him how important it was that he get his hands on them.

Malcolm told him he would get him the girls once they'd gotten rid of Thatcher. Once he was officially one of the Evolved, he would be able to sway the others to his cause by showing them the truth about the Creator and his precious Virtues.

Being with these people made him sick. He couldn't wait to destroy them all just to prove to the Creator that he wasn't as powerful as he thought.

The house was deserted when he returned. He wasn't sure where everyone went but decided to take advantage of the alone time. He wandered into the library, searching for the book he had heard so much about.

The fire was still burning, which led him to believe they left abruptly and hadn't been gone long. Looking around the library, he knew it would be nearly impossible to find the right book. Absalom thought he'd be able to find it because he is the same as The Evolved. But he had little reason to believe that to be true. In fact, Malcolm refused to compare himself to them in any way.

For Absalom to even say, that made him want to scream. His whole life had been dedicated to building a plan to get rid of them, now Abe wanted to compare him to them? As far as he was concerned, the Evolved were probably just as bad as the Virtues. They were all entitled. Entitled to whatever the Creator had decided for them. Well he wasn't going to be like that. He was going to decide for himself once he'd done what Absalom wanted so he could get the rest of his power.

He began searching the countless books on the shelf, but deep down, he knew they wouldn't have left it unattended. Malcolm began to thumb through one of the books and came across a section about Absalom. He settled down by the fire and began to read.

History of the Old Immortals:
Absalom

When the Old Immortals came to life, they were intended to be forces of good in a growing world. Absalom was born of darkness. From the very beginning, he was the bane of their existence. Absalom was full of trickery. His abilities were intended to bring mortals light and warmth, but he caused pain and panic wherever he went.

Absalom is the most dangerous and feared Immortal. Instead of creating sources of fire to help mankind, he created weapons to destroy them. Mountains became volcanoes, decimating entire civilizations. Natural pools of freshwater became hot springs with temperatures high enough to cook a human being in seconds.

After centuries of second chances, the Creator stepped in. Absalom was banished from the world and took to ruling the Under Realm. His other names are still used today. Most know him as Hades, Lucifer, and most commonly, Satan.

Malcolm sat up straight as the chills ran up and down his spine. He closed the book to see who had written this account. His eyes fell on a name he was familiar with from Absalom's own library, so he knew this was not a biased history for the Evolved.

This couldn't be right. He re-read the introduction and continued reading through the rest of the accounts. He slowly began to realize that he had literally made a deal with the devil.

Malcolm sat back with the book lying open in his lap. As he let the information sink in, he couldn't decide how he felt about what he'd learned. He knew Absalom was evil; here had never been any question about that. But it didn't matter because they shared the same goal: stopping the Evolved.

He couldn't shake the chill that had settled into his bones. The fire was still burning brightly as he pulled a blanket around his body and drifted into a fitful sleep.

Chapter Seventeen:
Hadley

Hadley was upset. No one had bothered to explain the vaguely ominous prophecy she and Whitley had received. Their mother seemed distant, so Hadley assumed she knew something more than she was letting on.

Right after they received their prophecies, Nora went off on her own. Hadley watched her leave and held Whitley back from following her. Thatcher had his head buried in his hands, still perched on the ruined columns. Kerr and Romulus had disappeared into the trees. It had been almost an hour of silence when Dorian made a comment about checking on Nora and headed down the path she'd taken. The girls sat facing each other at the ruined table with Tahlia between them.

Hadley cleared her throat and gave Whitley a weak smile before turning to Tahlia.

"Spill it, mom. What do you know?" Hadley asked all business.

"You two are a miracle," Tahlia replied reluctantly.

"Cut the crap. You should realize that we have part of you and part of dad, which makes us very difficult to avoid," Whitley said with an edge in her voice.

The Evolved

Tahlia looked at the girls, shaking her head. "I know. I can tell you all I know, but I don't know if it will help you. Because you are identical twins, you know you came from one egg. And because you are the only children to be born to a female of my kind, the power was not diluted. I believe you became twins because no single mortal, Evolved or not, could contain the amount of power I passed down to you."

The girls shared a confused look but encouraged their mother to continue.

"Because you were one egg, to begin with, and the two of you each hold half of my abilities, I am beginning to see how your prophecy will affect your future." Tahlia paused to look at each girl in turn. "Think about your prophecy and think about your lives. When have you ever been apart? The two of you have been inseparable since the day you were born."

Hadley wrinkled her forehead as she let the information sink in. "So, going from our prophecy, you think it means we can't ever be apart?"

Tahlia looked down. "More than that. I think you are still one person, only divided for the sake of survival."

She listened to her mother's words and felt them begin to sink into her body and mind. Hadley locked eyes with her sister and saw it all. They had always felt like two halves of a whole. They were alike in every way, but the extreme opposites in their personalities balanced the other out. The words of the prophecy rang in her head. "Although you are the same, you may go in different directions. But your greatest strengths appear when you are as one." If they were the same person in two bodies, what did that prophecy mean?

"So what are you saying, mom? That we aren't really two people? Are you telling us that we are going to go back to having just one body? How is that supposed to save mankind?" Whitley threw the words at their mother before turning to walk in the direction she saw Nora go.

Hadley knew deep down inside her what the prophecy meant. She had already worked it out in her mind. Both she and Whitley would have to part ways forever, or somehow become one. Either way, she would lose her sister.

Hadley looked at her mother and thought about how long she'd wanted to be with her. She reached across the table and took Tahlia's hand in hers as she thought about the implications of her role as one of the Evolved.

"Mom, do you think it was a mistake?" Hadley murmured.

"What are you referring to?" Tahlia replied.

"Having us," Hadley said slowly, as though each word caused her physical pain.

Abruptly, her mother looked up at her, holding her hand firmly. "No," she said while looking into Hadley's eyes. "No. It doesn't matter what the future holds, it doesn't matter what mistakes I've made in the past, and it doesn't matter that I didn't get to be part of your lives. You and your sister were never a mistake. You are both here as a result of the love Eric and I shared, and a result of the only selfish decision I ever made. I will never regret any of it."

She gathered Hadley into a fierce hug and kissed her forehead. Hadley knew this would be the response, but she needed to hear it. She knew her mother did not regret bringing them into this world, and she knew her mother loved both of them. The only thing she didn't quite understand was how her mother lived all these years, knowing that one of the twins would possibly die to save the world.

Hadley glanced at Thatcher. He had been sitting quietly in the same position through the entire exchange between them. She wondered what he was thinking. She couldn't even remember what his prophecy was. She walked over to him and sat on the ruined pillar next to him.

"Hey, you okay?" she asked, touching his shoulder.

"I'm fine. I don't really know how I should feel. This whole day has been insane," Thatcher responded without looking up.

"I know what you mean. Yesterday morning I never would have dreamed that I'd find my mother, let alone anything else that's happened," Hadley said quietly.

"I'm still not sure what to think about Dorian and leaving Malcolm behind," he said as he looked up at her. "I have to believe that the kid is innocent."

Hadley understood why Thatcher felt the way he did. Malcolm seemed nice enough, and he was just a kid. Hadley hadn't spent much time around him, and neither had Thatcher, but she knew his connection to

Malcolm was instant.

"I want to believe that too. But I don't know Malcolm. None of us do," Hadley said gently.

Thatcher nodded his head and tried not to look lost. "I'm just so torn right now. I want to believe that the Virtues know what they're doing, but what if they're wrong?"

Hadley realized she hadn't questioned the Virtues because they knew everything about her, they cared about her, and her mother was one of them. She had learned so much in the last twenty-four hours, and she knew it was right. She couldn't explain it, but she believed it.

"I don't believe they're wrong, Thatcher. They don't know what to make of Malcolm. He wasn't part of the plans they've had for centuries. And because he was talking to Absalom in the middle of the night, we're all a little worried," Hadley told him.

"Don't get me wrong, I'm worried about this whole situation too. I think I'm so upset about it because it could have easily been me. He's descended from Absalom, and so am I. His parents are dead, and so are mine. If he is working with Absalom, it could have easily been me that he chose. When I think about what that would mean for me, I know I have to find a way to help Malcolm," Thatcher responded.

She smiled at his words. She knew there was no way it ever could have been him working with Absalom. He had such a good heart, and she didn't think that came from being tossed from one foster home to another. It was something he'd inherited from his parents. She reached over and took his hand. He squeezed back and smiled at her.

"I'm going to take a walk," Thatcher said as he headed off in the same direction as Dorian.

Hadley could tell she was going to have to give Thatcher constant reassurance, and she realized she really didn't mind.

Chapter Eighteen:
Kerr

Even though he knew what his prophecy meant and what would happen to the others, he knew he couldn't tell them. His conversation with Romulus told him he had to leave this up to each person to choose their own way.

He paced back and forth in front of the tree stump where Romulus was perched. His grandfather smiled at him. He had already seen everything too.

"So, you're telling me I don't have a choice?" Kerr demanded

"I'm not telling you anything. You already know the answers," Romulus said.

"Well, what if I don't want to do what I saw? What if that's too much to expect of me? This is my life, too," Kerr cried in anguish.

"Is it really too much? Think about the glimpses you saw. How did you feel?" Romulus asked quietly.

Kerr was silent for a long time before he finally sat next to Romulus and said, "Happy. Happier than I ever thought possible. I felt love deeper than I ever thought was possible."

Romulus slapped him on the back. "Congratulations."

The Evolved

"The strange thing is, I know it's possible, and I actually do want it. But, I don't feel it right now. How do I get there?"

Romulus shrugged. "I fell for Anu the moment we laid eyes on each other. I don't know how it will be for you. Our abilities don't show us all the details, they just show us what can or will be."

Kerr heard a twig snap and turned to see Whitley walking down the path. He smiled kindly at her but quickly noticed the change in her demeanor. She was upset. He could feel her irritation and frustration pouring out of her.

"Are you okay?" Kerr asked.

"Don't bother asking a question you already know the answer to," Whitley replied dryly.

"Did you talk to your mom?" Kerr asked carefully.

"Yeah, and it's a load of crap if you ask me," Whitley shot at him.

"Whitley, I get it. I get it so much more than you can imagine." Kerr gently squeezed her shoulder.

"So, have you seen everything for everyone or what?" Whitley asked.

Kerr exchanged a troubled look with Romulus. He knew he couldn't say anything, and he really didn't have anything to say that would make her feel better.

"Whitley, it doesn't really work that way. I've seen bits and pieces of our futures, and all I can tell you is you will be okay. But you have to make your own choices."

Whitley nodded her head and quietly continued down another path in search of some solace.

Romulus came up behind Kerr and put his hand on his shoulder. Kerr stared out at the trees for a few more moments before turning to continue his questions.

"I think I should start by getting to know her," Kerr said matter-of-factly. "I haven't even read her yet. I was going to during dinner last night, but it felt like I was intruding. Is that weird?"

Romulus smiled and chuckled quietly. "See? You already feel the connection with her. Maybe it was love at first sight, you just didn't recognize it."

Kerr shrugged his shoulders. He thought back to the moment he first saw her. He'd been so preoccupied with everything else that was happening that he couldn't even pinpoint his initial reaction to her. He remembered looking at Nora at the dinner table and wanting to know more about her. He remembered making her angry when he said those hurtful things to Romulus. He remembered the strange way she responded to his jealous remarks. But he couldn't remember if there had been a deeper connection.

Nora. She was definitely beautiful. He leaned against a tree, thinking about her emerald eyes and wavy hair flowing down her back. He realized he had only heard her laugh once, but it was not the laughter that comes from happiness or humor, it was the laughter that came from incredulity. Nora. As he heard the words of his prophecy, he saw it all, felt it all, and could now admit that he wanted it all. He smiled as he thought about how he would act when he saw her next.

The Evolved

Kerr realized that without even spending any time alone with her, he was beginning to feel the love he'd glimpsed in his visions of the future.

"Look at me," he said to Romulus. "I've barely spoken to her, and I'm already falling in love, just thinking about what our future could hold."

"Now, you're talking! Just remember, this won't be as simple for her as it is for you. She doesn't know what you know. She hasn't felt it yet. You're going to have to take your time and let her get to know you before you try to jump in with both feet," Romulus warned. "But I know you can do it. You've got me and Dorian to help you win her heart."

Kerr nodded confidently, then closed his eyes. He let himself spend a few moments in the visions of the future; their first kiss, the moment she'd say yes, their marriage, and finally, their child. The beginning.

Chapter Nineteen:
Nora

Nora was angry. She had taken off running after the prophecies were done, and hadn't stopped even though she could feel Dorian behind her. She didn't know what she'd been expecting to hear when she received her prophecy, but it wasn't a cryptic message about being part of the future. She knew in her heart that being one of The Evolved may mean ushering in the New Era, but it also meant ending the lives of the three people who meant the most to her.

Her prophecy hadn't told her anything she didn't know. Of course, she thought she was the end, and of course the beginning of the New Era was coming from her, as well as the other Evolved. Ridiculous. That's what this whole prophecy nonsense was, ridiculous.

"Would you slow down?" she heard Dorian yell behind her.

She decided to disobey him for the first time in her life and pushed herself to run faster. It was liberating to run through those ancient trees. She continued to run without care until she felt the desperation in Dorian's pull behind her. She slowed her run to a jog, slowed her jog to a walk, and then stopped altogether. Dorian arrived behind her only a moment later.

"Look down," Dorian said with a hint of anger in his

voice.

Nora looked down and realized the ground opened to a vast ravine just beyond where she'd stopped. She rolled her eyes and turned to face Dorian.

"What do you want?" she asked icily.

"I need to talk to you," Dorian replied simply.

"About what? About this ridiculous prophecy, you just gave me? I have no interest in talking about it. I've already figured it out," she spat back at him.

"I don't think you did. It's not as simple as you think," Dorian said quietly.

Nora didn't understand how he could possibly be so calm and almost happy about this.

"You're going to die. What part of that don't you understand? I'm going to be responsible for ending your life and beginning the New Era. Somehow, even though there are five of us, it's all coming from me," she replied incredulously.

Dorian smiled warmly at her. "Like I said, it's not as simple as you think. First of all, you need to know that we are not going to die. We will simply become mortal."

Nora felt the tears welling up in her eyes. She wasn't going to lose them? Her family would still be there after all this; that thought alone was enough for her. A slow smile spread across her face as she lunged into Dorian's arms.

"You have a very important future, dear Nora, and I

need you to know I'll be here to support you every step of the way. We all will," Dorian said as he kissed her head.

"So, why will the beginning come from within me?" Nora asked. "There are five of us, aren't we supposed to do this together?"

"That, my dear, will be revealed to you in time," Dorian replied as he took her hand and began walking with her back toward the ruins. "We should probably get everyone back to the house, don't you think?"

As they walked back through the woods, they found Thatcher leaning against a tree.

"You guys ready to go? I want to get back and check on Malcolm. That kid is probably pretty freaked out since we left him all by himself," Thatcher said pointedly.

"I'm ready, we just need to gather everyone else up to head back," Nora replied.

Dorian walked ahead of them, sending out his calling to the rest of the group. Nora noticed Thatcher casting her sidelong glances as they made their way through the trees.

"What are you thinking about?" Thatcher asked her quietly.

"I really don't know what to think. I feel like the wind has been knocked out of me. I can hardly breathe," Nora replied honestly.

Thatcher nodded his head. "I think I know what you mean. I think my prophecy is about the kid. I have to help him break free from Absalom so he can choose the right path."

Nora nodded half-heartedly. She wasn't sure if he'd worked out the details correctly, just as she wasn't sure what her own prophecy could mean. But she knew it was important for Thatcher to keep an eye on Malcolm, whether he was meant to save him or not.

"I think the most important thing is that we all know that, no matter what, we're in this together. No matter what our prophecies mean, no matter what the future holds, we're all heading toward the same goal," Nora said as they made their way up a hill.

She took a moment to think about her prophecy now that she was able to clear her mind. She was not surprised that she was considered the heart. Her whole life, she'd been the only one of the Evolved to be at the heart of the situation, and now she was probably the one who would keep them all going. Nora knew that, no matter what her prophecy meant, she would gladly accept her role as the heart of the group.

They walked a few more minutes in silence before reaching the top of the hill where the ruins of the temple sat. Hadley, Tahlia, and Whitley were all standing together looking out over the mountainside; Tahlia had an arm around each of her daughters, which warmed Nora's heart. She looked to the other side of the clearing and saw Romulus and Kerr making their way down the hill. Nora smiled to herself at the sight of her aunt and uncle, finally spending time with those they held most dear. Once everyone arrived, she nodded to Dorian, closed her eyes, and focused on the library. The nausea was less than the last time she transported everyone, but she felt overwhelming exhaustion creeping over her.

Chapter Twenty:
Thatcher

As the library materialized around him, he was able to breathe again. He was looking right at Malcolm as they arrived and saw that the boy was holding a book. Thatcher knew it was his duty to protect Malcolm, so he quickly made his way to his side and gently lifted the book from his lap. He saw the page Malcolm had left off on, and read the information himself.

For the first time since joining this group, he realized the implications of being descended from Absalom and knew how deep the bond was that he and Malcolm shared. He put the book back on the shelf while everyone else regained their composure. Malcolm began to wake as the group began talking loudly about their time at the temple ruins.

He caught Malcolm's eye and indicated that he should follow him quietly. He saw Nora watching him with a strained face as he led the boy to the door. Thatcher led Malcolm down the hall away from the front entrance. He found a door and opened it, then allowed Malcolm to enter first. He heard everyone saying their goodnights in the hallway and waited patiently for the noise to die down before he turned to Malcolm.

"Okay, kid. Spill it," Thatcher said with his arms crossed.

The Evolved

"I don't think I know what you're talking about, dude," Malcolm replied, trying to sound cool.

"Don't play cute with me, Malcolm. I saw you. You were talking to that red-haired freak. You were talking to the guy Nora, and Whitley risked their lives confronting so they could save your butt," Thatcher whispered urgently.

He could tell Malcolm was fighting an inner battle, and he waited patiently to see which side won. He took a look around the room they had ended up in, realizing for the first time it was some kind of storage closet.

"Alright, fine. I was talking to my uncle, Absalom. So what? Aren't you the least bit curious to learn about the so-called 'red-haired freak' you and I are both related to?" Malcolm asked with a hint of sarcasm.

"Why would I want to know about him? His crazy brother tried to kill me!" Thatcher threw back.

"Absalom was not happy about that. He doesn't want Silas to kill you, he wants to meet you. We're his only living descendants," Malcolm answered indignantly.

"Yeah, and do you know why we're his only living descendants? Because he killed the rest!" Thatcher spat.

"Is that what they told you? Hmm, well, there are two sides to every story," Malcolm answered innocently.

"What the heck is that supposed to mean? It's pretty black and white. He's a maniac, killing everyone he can to get his hands on more power," Thatcher answered. "I saw the book you were reading. Absalom is the devil. Literally."

Malcolm turned white as a ghost for a few brief moments before regaining his composure. Thatcher knew he had surprised him by reading that page.

"That's just what Dorian and his gang of misfits want us to think," Malcolm pleaded. "Uncle Abe has always been there for me. He took me in after my parents died."

"Uncle Abe? You have got to be kidding me! We are talking about the guy who literally incinerated Kerr's father in the middle of a public sidewalk. He probably killed your parents and decided to keep you as a consolation prize. Maybe he thinks the older you are, the more power he can steal from you when he finally does you in!" Thatcher yelled.

Malcolm shook his head at Thatcher. He looked hurt and angry, tears welled up in his eyes.

"Oh yeah, Thatcher? And who killed your parents? Silas? Absalom? No. Maybe you should stop and think about how alike you and Absalom are before you start hurling insults at him." And with that, Malcolm flung the door open and took off running.

Thatcher was left reeling from the verbal slap he'd just received from Malcolm. From the moment he read the page in that book, all he could think about was how different he was from his ancestor. But now, he realized Malcolm could be right. Maybe he is just as bad as Absalom. Instead of having his parents taken from him like the other Evolved, he had been responsible for their deaths. He closed his eyes, blinking back the tears that were threatening to fall.

What was he doing here? He didn't fit in with this group. Malcolm fit in more than he did. He was a killer, just like Absalom. Maybe his concern for the kid wasn't really for Malcolm's well-being, but stemmed from the jealousy he felt at being close to Absalom; the only real family he had left. Maybe his prophecy really was meant for Malcolm; he was an orphan too. Malcolm had the ability to choose which path he was going to take, but it seemed Thatcher's was already laid out for him.

Before he composed himself enough to leave the storage room, he remembered something Dorian had said before he told him his prophecy. He remembered him saying he was a child of two descendants of the Old Immortals. What did that mean? He knew which parent came from Absalom as he remembered his father's bright red hair and bushy red beard, but who was his mother?

Maybe his path wasn't as concrete as he thought moments ago. If his mother was descended from the good side of the Old Immortals, maybe his soul wasn't as tainted as he feared. He took a deep breath and opened the door. When he did, he found himself staring into two deep brown eyes. Hadley. She smiled, sheepishly at him, and took his hand.

"I'm sorry for eavesdropping," she said genuinely.

"How much did you hear?" Thatcher asked in anguish.

"Everything." Hadley looked down at the floor briefly, then back into Thatcher's deep gray eyes. "You're not who he says, you know."

All at once, Thatcher pulled Hadley to him, then cupped her face in his hands as he kissed her deeply. He was pleased when Hadley wrapped her arms around him and returned his kiss ardently. The initial urgency of the kiss died down to a sweet embrace and a few gentle kisses. He pulled back slowly and looked down at Hadley with uncertainty. She smiled, stood on her tiptoes, and planted another quick kiss on his lips.

"That was nice," Hadley said quietly.

Thatcher laughed. "Just nice, huh?"

Hadley punched him playfully in the arm. "Well, you almost kissed me earlier, but you chickened out."

Thatcher took her hand and began to walk down the hallway with her. "I seem to recall more pressing matters at the time."

"Yes, well, with us facing imminent danger and all, we shouldn't let opportunities like that pass by us again." She winked at him as they made their way up the stairs to their rooms.

Thatcher walked Hadley to her door and gently kissed her. "I'll see you in the morning," he said as he turned back to his room.

"Goodnight!" Hadley called as she closed her door.

Thatcher walked into his room, closed the door, and threw himself on the bed. This had definitely been the weirdest day of his life.

Chapter Twenty-One:
Malcolm

Malcolm left the house in a hurry, afraid Thatcher would alert the others to his identity. He truly hoped Thatcher would follow him. He was supposed to be bringing him back to Absalom. As soon as he was outside, he shot up into the sky. He loved the freedom flying gave him. It was a freedom he could never be allowed on the ground. Absalom had always kept a short leash on him, but Malcolm always thought it was because he wanted to protect him. But after reading more about Abe, he wasn't so sure.

Maybe he only wanted him around so he could use him to get to the Evolved. As he flew over Newall, he couldn't help but wonder what was going to happen next. He had failed. He hadn't been able to get Thatcher to leave with him. He got so angry when Thatcher was attacking Absalom. Even if Absalom wasn't one of the good guys, he was the only family Malcolm really had. He continued out past the town to an old farm. He began his descent when he saw the large metal outbuilding that had become his home.

Absalom saw him coming, one of the abilities he'd stolen from Cole Mason. He was waiting outside when Malcolm landed.

"You were unsuccessful," he said simply.

"Well, maybe if you'd stayed away from that house, they wouldn't have mistrusted me so quickly," Malcolm said bravely.

"Do not question me," Absalom said menacingly.

Malcolm looked at the ground, unsure of what to say. He had never been so bold as to challenge Absalom, especially when it came to the decisions he made regarding the Evolved.

"I'm sorry," he said quietly.

"Follow me, boy. We have much to discuss," Absalom said as he turned and headed back into the building.

Malcolm followed him, feeling apprehensive about the conversation he was sure would be coming next. The outbuilding was large and open inside. It had once been used to store farm equipment but had long been abandoned. He and Absalom had moved in a few years ago, converting the storerooms into bedrooms, and using the wide-open space for training. He walked in to find Silas waiting on one of the couches in the corner. If they were both here, he was definitely in trouble.

"It's time you learned who you really are and why failure is not an option," Absalom told him, motioning for him to take a seat.

Malcolm sat down on the simple hard couch opposite the one Silas was perched on. He didn't want to be next to him if he was about to get punished.

"After meeting the Evolved, have you found yourself wondering why you are different from them?"

Absalom asked quietly.

"I guess I didn't really give it much thought. I assumed that you had chosen me based on opportunity, and that's what makes me different," Malcolm replied honestly.

"You're only partially right, child," Silas said with a sneer.

"Let me tell you a story about your mother, Malcolm," Absalom began.

Malcolm's interest was instantly piqued. He had never heard Abe talk about his parents, let alone tell him a story.

"Your mother was a quiet woman. She worked at a restaurant in a small town in Michigan. I'd been watching her for months. There was something about her that I couldn't place, but I was very curious," Absalom said the words with a hint of nostalgia.

"She had short dark hair, and her eyes were each a different color—one green, one brown. It was a strange sight to see. She was smart, and she was a single woman living in a small town with few options for mates. But she wouldn't settle for just anyone. She had many men show interest, but she never showed them the time of day." Absalom paused momentarily.

From the way Absalom spoke about Malcolm's mother, he got the impression that he actually cared about her. It made Malcolm lean forward, waiting for more information. He wondered if Absalom would tell him about his father too.

The Evolved

"I had not met anyone like her before in my entire existence. Sure, I'd taken wives before and produced children, but this was entirely different. I hadn't felt anything for those mortals. But your mother was different." Absalom glanced at Malcolm with a gleam in his eye. "I went into the diner a few times. Each time asking myself what I was doing there, but never being able to take my eyes off that woman."

Malcolm began to feel a thought creeping into his mind, but he didn't want to entertain it at all. He pushed it aside and waited silently for Absalom to continue.

"One night, there were no other customers for her to wait on, and she was there, talking to me. I ordered more food than I ever could have eaten just to see her. Eventually I asked her to sit down and join me. When she did, she laughed easily and smiled at me. I was completely taken with her. I asked her to see me outside of the diner, and she agreed." Absalom's voice was getting more strained the further he went into the story.

Malcolm finally allowed the nagging thought to break through as he realized where this story was heading. Absalom had actually loved someone, and that someone was his mother.

"As time passed, I became so consumed by your mother that I nearly forgot my mission in life. I still had duties to fulfill in order to stop the other Old Immortals from realizing the ridiculous prophecies the Creator had given them. But instead of taking care of business, I found myself lying with your mother in her room. I was completely obsessed with her. The way she made me feel was like nothing I had ever expected. I rolled over to face her and asked her to be my wife." Absalom sounded so sincere that Malcolm almost forgot who he was talking to.

"No. This doesn't make sense." Malcolm began to protest. "If you married my mother and she hadn't been with anyone else, that would make you my . . . "

"Father," Absalom finished the thought for him. "You are correct, Malcolm. You were never part of the plan. I knew that if your mother were to have my child, she would die. I had been very careful, trying to keep that from happening. Cassandra was a very passionate woman, and she loved me beyond anything I ever thought possible. As I said, I was completely consumed by our love, and despite being together for five years without creating a child, something terrible happened."

Malcolm was reeling from this new revelation. And it made him sick to think about it. Absalom had spent all these years hating him and blaming him for the death of his mother. He didn't know what to think about any of this. When he finally spoke again, it took Absalom completely by surprise.

"My mother's name was Cassandra?" he asked quietly.

"Yes," Absalom responded simply as though he didn't know what else to say.

"So you said something terrible happened. I suppose you mean me," Malcolm said numbly.

"Yes." He nodded. "Don't act so hurt, boy. I remember

it like it was yesterday. Your mother came to me with one of those stupid sticks and showed me that two lines meant we were going to be parents. I was angry. Not at her, but at myself. I couldn't believe I had done this to her. I'd seen my other wives suffer through their pregnancies and wasn't bothered by it. They were only a means to an end. But Cassandra was different. I was heartbroken, and I couldn't pretend my feelings matched hers. I left."

"You left her? Just like that? What did she do? Was she alone, did she die alone?" Malcolm felt his face growing hot as he thought of how selfish Absalom had to be to leave the woman he loved to suffer and die alone.

"Don't get ahead of yourself. I left her for two days. I was so terrified of what would happen that I couldn't bear to look at her. When I returned, she was elated and told me she had been so terrified that I wouldn't come back to her," Absalom said sadly. "It pained me to cause her such grief. I stayed with her through her pregnancy and cherished every moment with her until her heart stopped beating. I was going to kill you. I couldn't afford to have my own child become my downfall if you were to become one of the Evolved. I had a rock in my hand, ready to dash your brain out when you looked at me. You opened your eyes, and I saw the man your mother loved reflected there. I had to get away. I left you with Silas and Caprice after your mother died."

Malcolm was so shocked. He should be dead. His own father was going to smash his skull in with a rock. But Absalom seemed to have truly loved his mother; he had cared enough about Cassandra to leave her son with someone he trusted.

"I left and sought out one of the Evolved. I was gone for a few months, looking for Thatcher. I found his family and realized that he came from two of the descendants of the Old Immortals. His father came from me; I could see the resemblance. But his mother came from Dorian," Absalom said. "I watched through the window as his parents sang to him on his birthday, and I felt anger well up inside of me. I had never in my life felt jealous of someone else, but I knew at that moment that I was really angry because I would never share those moments with Cassandra. Our child would not have both of us, and that was my fault."

Malcolm was confused. He had always been told Thatcher killed his parents. He never knew Absalom had seen it happen. It made him sick, thinking about the conflict in what his father was telling him. He was so angry and hurt that he wouldn't get to be part of a happy family, so he just let that family die? He was really so jealous of his descendant and how happy he was that he just stood there? Malcolm was beginning to feel nauseated as he sat completely enraptured by the story of his parents.

"My anger filled me with hatred. Deeper hatred than I'd ever felt before. When Thatcher began to play with the flame and lit the plate on fire, I laughed. I laughed and used my abilities to encourage the flames. Soon, the whole house was engulfed in an inferno. The boy escaped, and his mother did as well, but I couldn't let her live. I grabbed her by the neck and threw her back into the flames," Absalom said with a self-satisfied grin.

Malcolm couldn't believe what he was hearing. Not only was Thatcher right about Absalom being a murderer, but he was also right about him being psychotic. His interest in the story of his mother had quickly changed to disgust upon hearing about what he did to Thatcher's parents and ultimately to Thatcher.

"You are a monster," Malcolm spat out.

"Careful, boy, he didn't kill you when he was grieving your mother, but he could kill you now. Or I could," Silas said menacingly.

"No, Silas, let the boy get it out," Absalom replied.

"You were going to kill a baby. Not just any baby, your own baby. When you couldn't kill me, you ran off and killed someone else. Thatcher has lived this whole time thinking it was all his fault, but really it was you. He was right, I shouldn't be here. I shouldn't be helping you. You are disgusting, and I won't help you anymore. I don't care if you kill me." Malcolm's voice rose to a shout.

In a flash, Absalom was in his face. Malcolm could see murder in his eyes. How had he never seen it there before? He had been so focused on getting revenge for the death of his parents that he believed every lie Silas and Absalom told him. After everything he read at Dorian's house, he knew he was, in fact, dealing with the devil. He didn't have to wait long to see what would happen to him as he began to feel his body temperature rise. The pain intensified and he doubled over, smoke coming from his mouth. It ended as quickly as it began, and he found himself on the floor.

"Never forget who you're dealing with, boy. If you are certain you will not help your father, your own flesh and blood, with the plans he has for you, then you will suffer. I will make sure you suffer good and long," Absalom hissed in his ear.

Chapter Twenty-Two:
Whitley

She woke in the morning to the sound of someone rapping on her door.

"Come in," she said groggily.

Hadley came in and shut the door behind her. The look on her face told Whitley she had something juicy to share.

"What's up?" Whitley asked with a yawn and a stretch.

"I kissed Thatcher," Hadley gushed.

"You what?! When?" Whitley asked, now wide awake.

"Last night. When we got back from the ruins, he took Malcolm off to talk to him, and I hung back to listen while everyone else went upstairs. Malcolm said some really harsh things and left. Thatcher opened the door of the pantry to find me standing there. I told him Malcolm was wrong about him and . . . " Hadley stopped and bit her lip.

"And what? Don't just leave me hanging like that, Had!" Whitley squealed.

"It happened so quickly. He just grabbed me and kissed me. It was pretty incredible, actually. Really intense." She shivered at the memory. "Then he walked me to my room, and I went to sleep."

The Evolved

Whitley smiled at her twin. She seemed really pleased with this development. Hadley had never been the type of girl to throw herself at a guy, but the way she'd been eyeing Thatcher was nothing short of obvious.

"Wait, Malcolm, left?" Whitley asked suddenly.

"Yes. He was mad at Thatcher for setting him straight about Absalom. Apparently, Malcolm was raised by that creep. He calls him Uncle Abe," Hadley told her.

"Wow. That's insane. Why would he raise him if he's been trying to kill all of us?" Whitley mused.

"I don't know. I don't have a very good feeling about it, though. It's a bit ominous. Anyway, I was thinking about going into town to grab some coffee today. We could meet dad there and bring him back here to talk everything over. I think it would be better if we show him we're free to come and go as we please since he's already apprehensive about all this," Hadley said.

Whitley had forgotten all about their father coming home. He was probably already home and wondering where they were. When they spoke with him the day before, they agreed to meet up with him as soon as he returned home. She blanched at the thought of him sending out a search party and dove for her cell phone. To her dismay, she had seven missed calls from their father.

"Hadley, have you checked your phone? I missed seven calls and ten text messages from dad," Whitley said nervously.

"I'll go check." Hadley left the room quickly.

Whitley got up and quickly braided her hair. It wasn't perfect, but it would have to do until she got home to shower and change. She hadn't brought anything with her, aside from her phone and her sister, so she was ready to go when Hadley returned.

"I have eight missed calls and six text messages. We should probably call him and just head to the house," Hadley said.

The girls had arranged to borrow Dorian's lime green car for the errand. Their mother was a little nervous about them leaving, especially after everyone knew about Malcolm, so she decided to tag along. As they pulled out of the driveway, Whitley could see the tension creep into her mother. This was definitely going to be an awkward reunion.

"Mom, don't worry, I'm sure he'll be relieved we're alright. He probably won't even notice you," Hadley said, trying to sound convincing.

"Gee, Had, that was helpful. Why don't you tell her you ran over her dog too?" Whitley retorted.

"I feel like a teenager going on a first date. I don't even know what will happen. Will he be mad? Will he be happy to see me? Will he even care?" Tahlia asked nervously.

Neither girl knew what to say, so they just stayed quiet. Whitley secretly hoped the appearance of their mother would lessen their father's irritation with them for taking off with a stranger.

As she drove through the country on the way back to Benton, she was surrounded by cornfields and cows.

The Evolved

Whitley remembered their first few days in this small town. She'd never seen so much corn in her life, and she'd never been so close to a cow that hadn't become a steak. The people of Benton were proud of their farming community, which often led the twins to feel out of place in conversations.

Soon, the silos gave way to civilization as she entered city limits. She drove down Maple Street, one of the main roads that crossed through Benton, on her way to the other side of the train tracks. Their large ranch was a little way out of town, near the lake. She knew their father would be pacing in his study waiting for them. He had been beyond irritated when she called him almost half an hour ago. Whitley conveniently neglected to tell him that they were bringing a surprise home with them.

Eric Callaghan was sitting on the front porch, waiting when they pulled into the driveway. He stood up and strode to the car, ready to give them a firm talking to. He stopped short as Tahlia stepped out of the car.

"Hello, Eric," she said shyly.

"Lia," Eric said breathlessly.

He looked as though he'd been punched in the stomach. It was almost painful to see the expressions that crossed his face as he stared at Tahlia. Whitley thought this moment would be tense and uncomfortable, but it was actually almost beautiful. Her father went from irate to speechless in only a few moments. She could see in the way he stood staring at Tahlia that he still loved her after all these years. Whitley and Hadley exchanged a meaningful look and stood to the side to watch their parents.

"Hi," Eric managed to say. He looked like a shy teenager.

"I've missed you," Tahlia said.

"I'm sorry I let you leave," Eric said. "I was scared. Then I thought the girls could live a normal life if you weren't there, so I didn't call you."

"You told them I abandoned them. How could you do that? I tried to see you all so many times," Tahlia replied.

"I don't know. I'm not proud of the choices I made. I thought I was protecting the girls." His words were sincere, and he was almost pleading with her to understand.

"I know. I forgave you a long time ago. I won't apologize for being who I am, but I am sorry I didn't tell you sooner," Tahlia told him.

"I would never ask you to be anyone else," Eric said with a sad smile.

"Awww!" Hadley gushed, ruining the moment.

Their parents turned to face them both. Eric looked embarrassed, and Tahlia looked relieved. Both girls smiled and hugged their parents fiercely. It was a moment they never would have expected, but it was a moment they all needed in order to put the past to rest. The four of them went into the large blue ranch house. The front door opened directly into the kitchen. The open floor plan continued onto a large living room with a stone fireplace. Their parents took

The Evolved

a seat on the large sectional that wrapped around the room. The girls excused themselves so they could take showers and change their clothes, leaving their parents to speak privately.

They went down the hall past the kitchen and took the stairs to the basement. Both girls were preoccupied with their thoughts as they headed into their bedrooms. Whitley smiled as she entered her bedroom. They weren't in trouble, and their parents were talking.

She felt like things were going their way as she stripped down in front of the bathroom mirror. Releasing her long blond hair from the braid, she examined her naked body. She didn't look any different than she had the morning before. She felt different, powerful, stronger, and complete. She was slim and had only slight muscle tone. Neither girl was athletic, but they were still small. Standing at about five and a half feet tall, she always viewed herself as average. She turned the shower on and stepped in as soon as it was warm enough. She felt the water soak into her hair and run down her back. She turned the water temperature a little higher and stood under the showerhead, massaging the shampoo and conditioner through her long thick hair. Once she finished washing her body, she turned off the shower and tied her hair up in a towel.

Whitley dried herself off, then chose some clothes from her walk-in closet and packed them in her large purple duffel bag. She grabbed some jeans and a gray hooded sweatshirt and got dressed. She pulled her hair into a messy bun. Once she finished packing the essentials, she headed out.

"Are you ready, Hadley?" Whitley called out to her twin.

"Yeah, just finishing packing. I can't decide what all I should bring with me. I guess we can always come back and grab more if we need to," Hadley said as she came out of her room wearing jeans and a pink sweater. She had done her hair in an intricate French braid that started on either side of her head and came together at the nape of her neck.

"Let's go see how it's going upstairs," Whitley said with a smile.

Chapter Twenty-Three:
Nora

Nora was alone in the sitting room, trying to get some quiet time. She wasn't sure what to think of Malcolm leaving. Thatcher had recounted the story to them over the breakfast table. His disappearance was troubling, but she knew it meant he hadn't done whatever it was that Absalom wanted.

Nora lay down on the deep window seat and closed her eyes. She hadn't slept well the night before, tossing and turning through countless nightmares. They were all different, but ended the same way, with her standing over Dorian's dead body. The door opened, and someone came in. She took a peek under her arm and saw Kerr approaching the window.

"Hey," he said as he sat down near her feet.

"Hey," she replied sleepily.

"How are you doing?" Kerr asked even though he already knew the answer.

"Not great. I feel like I've had a rug pulled out from under me, and I just keep falling rather than hitting the floor," she told him with her eyes closed.

"Why do you feel like that?" Kerr asked, sounding sincerely interested.

The Evolved

"I just feel like everything I thought I knew about the Old Immortals is wrong. My head is full of questions, and I don't know which one will give me the answer I need."

Kerr nodded at her. She wasn't sure what to make of him. He clearly had a good conversation with Romulus after he received his prophecy. She decided he was probably the only one in the group who didn't seem completely lost. Maybe it was because of his gift, or maybe it was because he knew he could trust the Old Immortals.

"Do you want to get out of here?" Kerr asked her.

"Where would we go?" Nora asked, sitting up.

"I thought it would help if we got our minds off all this and maybe went to grab some ice cream?" Kerr said, hopefully.

"I would love that!" Nora said, jumping up. "I haven't been into Benton in a while. We should go to Dairy Barn!"

Kerr laughed and followed her as she excitedly left the sitting room.

"We're going out!" she yelled to Dorian and Romulus. "We can take my car! You'll love it."

Nora had a red Mini Cooper. Dorian had let her purchase it when she graduated high school so she could drive to the University of South Dakota when she needed to attend classes on campus. Kerr smiled when he saw the car and hopped into the passenger seat. Nora decided she was going to get to know Kerr.

She couldn't believe he had lived in Benton the whole time and she never knew he was there. It just proved how sheltered her life had been. She knew it was because Dorian wanted to keep her safe, but she would have liked to at least known another Evolved was living so close to them. She pulled into a parking spot at the Dairy Barn and put the car in park.

"Do you want to eat here or take the ice cream somewhere else?" he asked her.

"Let's take it to go, and I'll show you my favorite place in Benton," Nora said with a sly smile.

They went inside and ordered two Chocolate Peanut Butter Mudslides to go. She explained that her favorite place was only a short walk from the Dairy Barn, and led the way down the street.

"I've lived here for a long time, and I have no idea where we're going. Is this a secret spot?" Kerr teased her.

"No, it's just a place I used to go when I needed to clear my mind. I didn't have any friends because I was ahead of my age. The kids in my grade didn't like me because they thought I was too young, and the kids my age didn't like me because I was smarter than them," Nora replied simply.

"That is really sad. I didn't have any friends because I didn't want them," Kerr said.

Nora led him down the road and turned on to one of the bike paths by the river. She slowed, so they were walking next to each other and began to ask him questions about his past.

The Evolved

"So, how was growing up with your mom and stepfather?" she asked conversationally.

Kerr shrugged. "It was alright. My stepdad is a good guy, and I love my mother. I missed my dad, and no one could ever take his place, except maybe Romulus. But Andrew, my stepdad, takes good care of my mom and treats me with respect. I can't complain."

Nora nodded. "I wonder what it would have been like to grow up with my parents. Even just one of them. I don't even know what they looked like. That's why I told you you're lucky. You got to be with at least one parent. And you got to be with your Evolved parent long enough to remember him."

Kerr looked at her in surprise. "I was so busy thinking you were lucky because you got to grow up knowing about our history, and knowing that something was expected of us, even if you didn't know what it was."

They fell into a comfortable silence as they continued down the path. Just before the path went uphill, Nora turned and started to lead Kerr into the grass. She had stumbled upon her hideaway when she was sixteen. She remembered it clearly because it was one of the first times Dorian let her go into Benton without him. He told her that because she was a high school graduate, she deserved certain freedoms, and one of those was to go to the Dairy Barn to get them all ice cream. On one such trip, she decided to take a walk in the park. She'd gone to sit by the river's edge and happened to look at the bridge to her right. She was curious and went to explore. Nora found the area under the bridge hidden behind tall reeds and cattails.

There was a cemented area that she could sit down in. Every time she went to Benton, she would make a special trip to this spot.

They arrived at the reeds and cattails, which she pulled aside to allow room for Kerr to enter. She stepped in after him and smiled at the paintings covering every inch of concrete.

"Wow. This is stunning. Did you do this?" Kerr asked her in surprise.

"Yes. I love to paint. This is basically the story of the Old Immortals. Here is the Creator, and over here is the stone temple. I know it doesn't look right, but I'd never been there before today. This is a scene from Greece, and here's Egypt." Nora was so excited to finally show someone her work that she wondered if she'd overloaded Kerr with information. He was quietly staring at the paintings.

"This is beautiful. I can't believe you did all this, and no one has ever tried to get rid of it. I am so . . . " He stopped talking and drew in a sharp breath. "This is Anu."

Nora nodded at him and felt her cheeks turning red. She had never shown anyone her artwork.

"I painted the first moment they met, their wedding day, and the birth of their son, Keiran," Nora told him.

Kerr hadn't taken his eyes off Anu.

"Nora, this is just amazing. You are so talented. Did you paint these based on stories you've read?" Kerr asked her.

"Yes. I have heard them so many times they have come to life in my mind," Nora said.

"This is beautiful, really. You are so talented," Kerr said.

Nora smiled again and continued to show him the various scenes she had painted. She could tell Kerr was genuinely interested in her artwork. It was a bit of a novelty to have someone show interest in this part of her life. Of course, Dorian was proud of her, but it was always secondary to her Evolved abilities. Sharing this with someone else made her nervous, but Kerr made her see how special she really was.

Chapter Twenty-Four:
Kerr

Climbing back into the red Mini Cooper, Kerr couldn't shake the feeling that something was off. He kept shooting sidelong glances at Nora, half expecting her to be upset about something. But the only reading he was getting from her was happiness. He knew she'd never shown anyone her artwork and was pleased by his reaction.

As they made their way back to Dorian's house, he found himself experiencing despair so deep he felt short of breath. He started gasping as he desperately tried to get air in his lungs. Kerr didn't know why, but he was certain he was having a panic attack.

"You okay?" Nora asked him as he attempted to calm himself.

Kerr shook his head and looked out the window. He didn't trust his voice. He groaned and grabbed his stomach as the feeling began to affect him physically. Doubling over from the pain, Kerr cried out.

"Kerr! What's wrong?" Nora asked as she pulled to the side of the road.

Kerr opened the door and flung himself onto the ground. He heaved into the ditch next to the dirt road. Nora went around the car to check on him but had to turn away as she saw him throwing up. Kerr hadn't experienced a pain like this since his father died; it was physical and emotional. He choked back a sob as another wave of nausea hit him.

"Kerr?" Nora said uncertainly. "I'm going to transport you home, then come back for my car."

He nodded and tried to sit up. He felt Nora's hand on his shoulder as the world began to spin. When he opened his eyes, he found himself curled in a ball on the floor of the foyer. He heard Nora call for help and saw Romulus' feet approach him. Strong hands helped him sit up again, and he soon found himself staring into the deep blue eyes of Romulus.

"You're going to be alright, son," Romulus told him.

"It hurts so much. I can't even move," Kerr replied.

"Close your eyes. Focus on the pain," Romulus told him.

"No way," Kerr told him.

"You have to, Kerr. It will consume you if you don't," Romulus said firmly.

Kerr thought carefully, focusing on the source of the pain. He imagined himself burrowing past the nausea and colliding with the pit of his stomach. Once he was face to face with the source of his grief and physical pain, he saw the horror unfolding in front of him.

He was standing in the middle of an unfamiliar street. He momentarily wondered if he had gone deaf. There were no sounds. There was nothing. The town looked completely deserted. He took a few steps forward, looking for any sign of life. He caught sight of a small child running around the corner a few buildings up. Kerr started running toward the child, desperate to figure out what was happening. The closer he got, the deeper the feeling of dread and emptiness was. He covered his face to keep himself from breathing in the acrid smell that hit him like a ton of bricks. He couldn't breathe; his lungs were aching from lack of oxygen.

As he rounded the corner, he stopped short and stared in revulsion at the scene in front of him. There were bodies everywhere. Hundreds of bodies lying in the street. What was happening?

He saw the child ahead of him, leaning over one of the dead. Kerr approached the little girl slowly, stopping when he saw the state of the body in front of him. The child paid him no attention, it was obvious he was just an observer of the scene. The woman was breathing, but only just. It looked as though her skin had been peeled off. Her clothing was gone. The girl leaned closer as the woman tried to speak.

Kerr grimaced at the horrific sound that came from her lips; it sounded like a wet gurgle. She took a few shallow breaths before lying still. Kerr took a step back and looked around desperately. Each body he saw was in the same state as this woman, but there was no sign of a fire.

Kerr was torn away from the scene by the sound of a laugh behind him. He turned quickly and saw Silas and Absalom approaching the child. Kerr tried in vain to warn the little girl.

"Well, hello, child," Silas said in a lilting voice.

The Evolved

"I can't find my mommy," the little girl replied.

"No, I can't imagine you will," Silas told her with a sneer.

The girl looked around at all the death and destruction and began to cry. Kerr stepped forward, wanting to comfort her, but he knew it would be no use. Absalom was wandering around, admiring his handiwork with ill-contained glee.

"I haven't had this much fun in years," Absalom told his brother as he rested a hand on the head of the little girl.

Kerr cringed at the casual contact he made with someone so innocent.

Silas nodded. "We haven't done this much destruction in years."

"True. And to think, this would all have been solved if those silly Evolved had given themselves up to us, and this little girl wouldn't be an orphan," Absalom said as he crouched down by the girl.

The child looked at him with wide tear-filled eyes. She didn't look to be any older than four or five. Kerr silently hoped the Old Immortals would find some piece of their original purpose within themselves and spare the girl. But he knew his hope was futile. Kerr could see what was coming before it happened. He dropped to his knees next to the girl and tried to shield her from Absalom. Although the child could not see him, he wrapped his arms around the little girl and held her close.

"Well, there's no point in letting another orphaned child suck the life out of the world, is there?" Absalom asked Silas casually.

The silent agreement that passed between them told Kerr the girl was on borrowed time. Kerr closed his eyes as the screaming started. He couldn't bear to see that beautiful little girl become like those around her.

Kerr collapsed to the ground. He cried freely and shrank away as Romulus tried to comfort him. While he was gone, Nora must have returned because he caught the scent of her shampoo as she enveloped him in a comforting embrace. He collapsed into her and clung to her shirt.

Kerr opened his eyes. He looked around the room, realizing that someone had brought him to his bedroom. He could see the bookshelf wall across from his position on the bed. He started to roll over but realized he wasn't alone. He looked up to find Nora staring down at him. His head was lying in her lap.

"Hey," she said quietly.

"Hey," Kerr said as he cleared his throat and sat up. "Sorry."

"It's okay. When you took hold of me in the foyer, you were delirious. You wouldn't stop crying. Romulus tried to talk to you, but you kept telling him to go away. You wouldn't let anyone touch you but me." Nora looked at him with concern.

"I don't remember," Kerr replied. As he closed his eyes and tried to remember what had led up to this moment, he felt his stomach turn. Every memory, every moment came rushing back to him. He got up quickly and headed for the door.

"Come on, I have to talk to the others. They need to know what happened." Kerr threw caution to the wind and grabbed Nora's hand. He pulled her down the stairs, and they found everyone sitting in the breakfast nook. Romulus jumped to his feet. Dorian and Thatcher gave him confused looks. He looked around and realized the twins and Tahlia hadn't returned yet.

"Kerr, I know what you were feeling. I felt it too. I haven't felt one like that since September eleventh. And prior to that, the Holocaust," Romulus told him. "But I've never experienced anything like what you did. What did you see?"

Kerr recounted his vision to the group. Nora stayed by his side through the whole description. When he finished, his voice was raw from unshed tears. Thatcher was staring at him in disbelief. Dorian had buried his face in his hands.

"I've never witnessed one of their despicable acts, I've only had the feeling of dread. I knew something was coming, but I never saw it. I'm so sorry you had to experience that, Kerr," Romulus told him.

"This is seriously messed up. I mean, I read about Absalom in that history book, but I never fully believed it. He really is the devil," Thatcher said in disgust.

"To mistake him for something that simple would be terribly misguided," Dorian told Thatcher.

"We need to go there. What if it hasn't happened yet?" Kerr asked desperately.

"I agree. We can't take any chances. Perhaps you were shown that child so you could prevent her fate," Dorian told him.

"I'm going," Thatcher said automatically.

"I have to be there. I won't be able to live with myself if I don't go," Kerr said.

"Then it's settled. We're all going," Nora told them.

"I will stay behind in case Tahlia and the twins return," Dorian said.

"Kerr, I need you to focus on that street. Remember your surroundings. Think about the buildings, the street. I'm going to try to transport us there from your memory," Nora told him.

Kerr nodded. "It was a small town. There were old brick buildings on both sides of the street. Light posts lined the sidewalks that ran in front of the businesses. I remember seeing a faded sign painted on the side of a building; it was blue and white, and it was for Rexall . . . "

The room began to spin, and as it stopped, Kerr knew they had arrived. He was staring right at the advertisement on the side of the building. But something was different. Instead of the silence he had encountered in his vision, screams and shouts were echoing off the brick buildings.

Chapter Twenty-Five:
Thatcher

All around, people were running in the street, yelling at each other to hide. Thatcher glanced at Kerr and saw the confusion he felt reflected on his friend's face. This must have been an extreme contrast to his vision. They looked at each other for a moment before Kerr took off running toward the end of the street. Nora, Thatcher, and Romulus followed in his wake. When they got to the end of the street they were faced with a terrifying sight. The destruction had already begun. People were falling to the ground around them. One minute they were standing there, the next they were screaming and falling to the ground. All that was left of their bodies was a sticky shell of human remains. Some of them were still alive when they fell to the ground, but they were beyond repair; all that was left to do was die.

"We have to help them. We have to stop this," Nora said.

Kerr was looking around, desperately trying to catch sight of the little girl who was haunting his thoughts. Romulus had a heartbroken look on his face as he watched the destruction unfold. Thatcher wondered if he would see Malcolm helping Silas and Absalom. A woman pushing a stroller ran into the alley, stopping

The Evolved

short when she caught sight of them.

"Who are you? You're not from here. Are you with the strangers? Please don't hurt my baby!" She sobbed.

"Shhh! Ma'am, you're right, we're not from here. We came to help, but we need to be quiet," Romulus told the woman. She seemed to calm at his words.

"How can you help? How can anyone help? Everyone is dying. My husband . . . My daughter . . . " She choked on her words.

Thatcher looked at Nora. She seemed to be fighting an inner battle. She kept looking between the woman and Romulus, then frantically glancing at the mouth of the alley.

"Nora?" Thatcher asked.

"What, Thatcher?" she snapped at him.

"Do it," Romulus said suddenly.

"Do what?" Thatcher asked, thoroughly confused.

"Nora, you have to. The risk of exposure is nothing compared to saving the lives that will be lost here if we don't help," Kerr told him.

"Someone catch me up," Thatcher said, shrugging apologetically at the woman.

"I'm going to get them out of here," Nora said simply. Then she smiled at the young woman in front of her. "What's your name?"

"Penny."

"Penny, I'm going to help you. I'm going to get you and your baby out of here. You have to trust me. Can you do that?" Nora asked quietly.

The woman furrowed her brow, but nodded and checked on the baby. Nora leaned forward as she put her hand on Penny's back.

"Find more people, and bring them here. I'll be back soon." And with that, she disappeared.

"You two should get people here. I'm going to distract Absalom," Thatcher said.

Romulus and Kerr exchanged a look of concern.

"You can't talk me out of this. I am the only one here who has an ability that can do anything against him. You two can sense people. It's a no-brainer, really," Thatcher told them.

Thatcher felt mildly uncomfortable as Romulus placed both hands on his shoulders and looked him in the eyes.

"You have nothing to prove, Thatcher. Don't forget that," Romulus said before heading out of the alley. Kerr slapped Thatcher on the back and followed the Old Immortal.

Thatcher took a deep breath and was about to leave the alley too when Nora reappeared.

"Where'd they go?" Nora asked.

"They just went to find more people. I'm going to go offer myself up on a silver platter," Thatcher said cheekily.

The Evolved

"You're what?!" she almost shouted. "Are you crazy? You have no idea what you're doing. You're not ready for that."

"I have to, Nora. Malcolm left yesterday. He left and went back to them. I have to see if he's with them. I have to see if he's helping them do this to these people. But most of all, I have to face Absalom," Thatcher told her firmly.

Nora was quiet for a moment. She bit her lip and looked at Thatcher thoughtfully. When they heard footsteps approaching, she nodded her head at him and told him she understood. Kerr had arrived with three more people: a scared old woman, and two terrified teenage boys. Nora didn't even bother explaining this time, she simply grabbed onto them and disappeared.

Thatcher and Kerr left the alley together. Kerr was still searching the streets for the little girl from his vision.

"Maybe she hasn't lost her mother yet, Kerr. Let me try to distract the Old Immortals while you look for her," Thatcher told him.

"Romulus is right, you know. Just because your prophecy tells you that you are torn doesn't mean you have something to prove. You are who you are, and who you are is one of us," Kerr told him as he jogged across the street.

Thatcher stepped out into the afternoon sunlight. If he only looked at the sky, he could almost forget what was happening around him. But the pungent odor and endless tortured screams continued to remind him where he was. He was in Absalom's playground. Thatcher wasn't sure what he was supposed to be confused about. He wanted to stop Absalom with all his heart and all his mind. He knew, without a doubt, his prophecy was not about that.

After hearing a scream erupt to his left, he took off in that direction. He broke through a row of bushes beside a parking lot to find Absalom standing over a fleshless body. It was obvious that the scene around him was something Absalom enjoyed. He didn't blink twice at the bodies lying on the ground around him; he almost looked happy.

Thatcher stepped out from between the bushes. He had seen enough death and destruction today. He needed to distract Absalom and find Silas.

"What's up, Hades?" Thatcher shouted.

Turning in slow motion, Absalom's lips curled into a devilish smile.

"What was that?" Absalom asked.

"I don't recall stuttering," Thatcher shot back.

"Well, Thatcher, fancy meeting you here," Absalom replied with an almost pleasant smile.

"Surprise!" Thatcher said with his arms spread wide. "Where's that boyfriend of yours?"

"Oh, now we've never even been properly introduced, and you're already insulting me?" Absalom chided.

"So, is all this your handiwork?" Thatcher asked.

"Yes, lovely, isn't it?" Absalom asked. "It takes a

certain amount of self-control to burn the flesh from someone's body without killing them. Luckily, I've had a lot of practice."

Thatcher couldn't believe how casually he spoke of such awful things. He wished Silas was here too so he could be certain the killing had halted altogether. He needed to think of what to say to keep Absalom from moving on.

"Where's Malcolm?" Thatcher asked without thinking.

"He's sleeping. He'll probably be sleeping for a while," Absalom told him. Something in the way he said the words made Thatcher think there was more to his statement.

"I can't believe he would want to miss out on the party you've been throwing here," Thatcher replied.

"Well, this was never really his thing. Silas and I tend to do the maiming. Malcolm tends to pull the innocent act to bait gullible people," Absalom remarked.

"Ouch. Is that what he told you? That I'm gullible?" Thatcher asked. "Well, rest assured, Absalom, I never once fell for his lines about you. I see you for what you really are. I know you hold nothing but darkness inside you, and you deliver nothing but pain and suffering."

"Nice speech, boy."

Thatcher heard the voice behind him before he had time to react. Silas had appeared from between the row of bushes. He looked just as broody as ever. Thatcher backed up and turned his body, so the three of them formed a triangle. There was no way he was going to let them sneak up on him again.

"Well, Silas! I haven't seen your brand of crazy in a while," Thatcher said with a smile. "How long has it been?"

Silas growled quietly as he took a step forward. "You're a cheeky little bastard, aren't you?"

"Now, Silas, don't rub in that he doesn't have a father. You know that's a sore subject for him," Absalom scolded his brother.

Thatcher felt the heat rise in his face. Absalom knew just how to get to him. It made him angry that something so simple could affect him so much. He didn't want the Old Immortals to see his weaknesses.

"You know, boys, I lost my father long ago. But didn't you lose someone a little more recently, Silas?" Thatcher asked.

The ground rumbled under his feet. Silas was angry. He knew he was taking a huge risk, but he was getting a little desperate. He wasn't sure why the conversation had gone on so long without a fight. What did they want from him?

"Thatcher, it's a shame you didn't decide to return with Malcolm. I had such high hopes for you," Absalom said.

"Oh yeah? Like what?" Thatcher asked.

"Well, I would have liked for you to join me. If you had, I would have given you the honor of doing away with Malcolm. You could have absorbed his abilities and ruled beside me when I destroy the Evolved and the Virtues," Absalom replied.

"Right, then you could have killed me when you were done using me," Thatcher replied. His heart rate was increasing. Had Absalom just admitted to killing Malcolm?

"You know me too well." Absalom laughed.

"So, because you didn't give me the honor of killing Malcolm, I take it you'll hold that honor?" Thatcher asked him.

"Oh, do you still have a soft spot for the boy who betrayed you?" Absalom asked.

"Why don't we just kill him?" Silas demanded.

"We can't do that, Silas. He hasn't served his purpose yet," Absalom said cryptically.

"Guys, I'm standing right here," Thatcher said. "Look, it's been nice, but if we're not going to fight or anything, I might as well be heading home."

"Oh, don't be ridiculous. I said I wasn't going to kill you, but that doesn't mean we can't have a little fun." Absalom smiled cruelly.

Before Thatcher had time to react, thousands of tiny ice shards hit his body. Each shard sliced his skin easily, leaving him to drip blood on the ground from multiple wounds. He formed a flame in the palm of his hand and sent it flying toward Silas. His opponent was quicker than he expected and managed to twist out of the way before he was hit. Silas was laughing as Absalom took his turn. He wiggled his fingers and shot tiny flames toward Thatcher.

Thatcher dropped to the ground in time to only be hit by a few of the tiny fireballs. He tried to get back up but realized he was lightheaded from blood loss.

He had to work with what he had. From his position on the ground, he focused his energy on the Earth's core. He tapped into the liquid heat, flowing deep underground and imagined it breaking through the ground. As each fountain of lava shot from the ground, it encircled the Old Immortals.

It bought Thatcher enough time to call out to Nora before he lost consciousness.

Nora appeared by his side. She looked between Thatcher and the Old Immortals for only a brief moment before she grabbed his arm, and the world began to spin.

Chapter Twenty-Six:
Nora

Nora had gotten thirty people to safety, but Kerr still hadn't found the little girl from his vision. Romulus was unable to find any more survivors. He had taken to sitting with the dying in their last moments. Nora watched him with tears in her eyes. She was in awe of the care he showed to these poor suffering souls.

Nora felt a pull in the pit of her stomach. She thought it was just the emotions and fear she had been experiencing since they arrived, so she tried to ignore it. But the pull got more intense, and she realized she could hear Thatcher calling her name. The pull started again, and she let herself be taken with it. Nora opened her eyes to find herself facing Silas and Absalom. They were surrounded by liquid fire. It weaved around them as though they were encaged. Nora looked between them, then down at her feet.

"I can't hold this much longer. They're too strong," Thatcher told her. He was covered in blood, but she couldn't discern where it was coming from. "I'm losing control. We need to leave."

Without another thought, Nora grabbed Thatcher's hand and took him home. Dorian looked up in surprise when she arrived without Kerr and Romulus. But his surprise quickly changed to concern when he saw Thatcher.

"What happened to him?" Dorian asked as he came forward.

"Silas and Absalom. I have to get back. Without Thatcher there, they're free. They'll find Romulus and Kerr in no time," Nora told him. The distress in her voice was evident.

Dorian hoisted Thatcher to a standing position and carefully put an arm around his waist. Nora was worried about Thatcher, but she had to get back. She apologized to Dorian, then found herself back in the alley. Neither Kerr nor Romulus was there, and the screaming had stopped.

If the screaming had stopped, there was probably no one left to scream. Nora crept along the brick wall to her right. There was something about the overwhelming silence that made every move seem like a sonic boom. Once she reached the alley opening, she swept her eyes across the scene in front of her. Clearly, Silas and Absalom had increased their efforts as soon as they were free of Thatcher's cages. There were bodies everywhere now. No one was moving. Where were Kerr and Romulus?

Out of the corner of her eye, she saw a little girl run around the corner. She was small, and she wore jeans and a pink jacket. Her shoes lit up as she ran. The little girl looked around in fear before she came up to Nora. Crouching down so she would be at the little girl's height, Nora smiled kindly at her.

"Hi, honey. My name is Nora. Who are you?" Nora asked quietly.

"Sophie," she replied in a tiny voice.

"Sophie, where is your mommy?" Nora asked her.

"I don't know. She was here, but when the bad men came, I lost her. My daddy is hurt. Can you help him?" Sophie told her.

Nora gave her a small smile and took her hands. "Where is your daddy?"

The little girl pointed down the block. Nora looked in that direction and saw Silas and Absalom making their way down the road. Absalom saw someone struggling to move and stopped to snap her neck. When he stood up, he looked right at Nora. Even from this distance, she could see the wicked smile on his face.

"Sophie, listen to me. Did your daddy look like these people around us?" Nora asked, hating herself for making the innocent little girl look at the bodies littering the street.

Sophie started crying and nodded her head when her eyes fell on the body closest to them. Nora pulled her close and kissed her head. When she looked up, she saw Kerr and Romulus running around the corner. A look of relief crossed Kerr's face as he saw the little girl in her arms.

"We need to get out of here," Nora told them when they approached.

"There are no more survivors," Romulus replied sadly.

The Evolved

A wall of fire shot up down the middle of the street, and the building next to them burst into flames. Nora closed her eyes with her arms around the little girl. She felt Kerr and Romulus each place a hand on her shoulder as she focused on transporting them to the same place she took the other survivors.

"Sophie!" she heard a woman cry out.

"Mommy!" Sophie yelled as she ran in the direction of Penny, the woman with the stroller she had first saved.

Kerr smiled at Nora and Romulus. The relief in his face was evident. Nora looked around the room at the traumatized people she brought here. She had brought them to a safe house belonging to one of their scouts. No one said anything about how they arrived or about what they had seen. Nora didn't know how they were going to explain everything these people had witnessed.

"Can I have your attention, everyone?" Romulus said.

When the whole room turned their attention to him. He cleared his throat and made his way to the middle of the group.

"I'm sure you're all confused and scared. No one should have to witness, endure, or experience the things you saw today. You don't know us, and you have no reason to trust us. But I need you all to understand something." Romulus paused. When he saw that he still had their undivided attention, he continued, "There are many horrible things that happen in our world. Men are responsible for some, but other things are not as easily explained. The truth is, there is no easy explanation for what you witnessed today."

"You're angels!" Sophie exclaimed as she ran to Nora's side and took her hand. "You saved us from the bad men. You brought me back to my mommy."

Nora felt her heart melt as the little girl smiled up at her with love and awe. She squeezed Sophie's hand. Romulus smiled at her innocence and continued his speech.

"We have brought you all to a safe house where those men will not find you. The official story you will hear from the government and news reports will be that there was a gas leak or an explosion," Romulus told them. "You will know that is not the case, but it is easier for the world to believe that story. I only ask that you carry in your hearts the people you have lost. We were sent to save you, but we were too late to save you all. I am deeply sorry."

The survivors spoke amongst themselves for a few moments. A few were crying silently, holding onto each other for comfort and support. One man stepped forward, looking Romulus in the eye.

"You're right, we don't know who you are. But what little Sophie said is true. You saved us. I know a miracle when I see one. No one would believe us if we told them otherwise," the man finished and shook Romulus' hand. "Thank you."

Nora watched the people she had saved through the tears in her eyes. She couldn't imagine what they were going through. The town was very small, but they had only about a third of their population remaining. She looked at Kerr and saw the same sorrow she felt reflected in his face. She linked her arm through his and leaned her head on his shoulder.

"We should go," Kerr whispered to her.

"Yeah, but how will they get home?" Nora asked.

"We're not too far from their home. The scout will take care of everything," Romulus explained.

Nora nodded and grabbed Romulus' hand. They faded away and found themselves standing in the foyer of Dorian's house.

Dorian came out of the kitchen. The relief was written all over his face. He pulled Nora into a tight hug, then shook hands with Romulus and Kerr.

"Thatcher had a lot of minor cuts, but only three were deep. He lost a lot of blood, but he'll be alright. Hadley, Whitley, and Tahlia came back shortly after you left. They took him to the hospital in Benton," Dorian told them.

"Thank you, Dorian," Nora said as she stepped forward to hug him.

They made their way to the kitchen and sat down. Romulus excused himself to wash his hands. Nora suspected he had held the hands of some of the dying. Once they were seated, Kerr and Nora shared their story with Dorian.

"They're getting braver. They haven't done this much destruction in years. It was bold to do something so public. The survivors have complicated things for them. They're likely to become reckless," Dorian told them.

"What do we need to do?" Kerr asked.

"We need to train. We need to be prepared for any of us to take them on at any moment," Dorian told them.

Nora knew their lives were getting more complicated, and she didn't know what that would mean for them. She closed her eyes and laid her head on the table. No matter what, she would be ready the next time she came face to face with Silas and Absalom.

Chapter Twenty-Seven: Dorian

Dorian, Romulus, and Tahlia spent hours every day training the Evolved to control their abilities. They spent very little time working with them on any physical training. The chances of them getting close enough to either Silas or Absalom to engage in hand to hand combat were slim.

When they weren't training, the Evolved were getting to know each other better. Dorian had noticed Thatcher and Hadley's budding relationship. He was pleased to see that Kerr had taken the initiative to spend time alone with Nora. Whitley spent a lot of time with her mother, making up for lost time.

He watched as all the pieces began to fall together and wondered how long it would be before Silas and Absalom came around for another visit. Dorian took a deep breath in the crisp October morning. He sipped his tea while he watched Whitley and Hadley practice their abilities in the backyard. Their early morning battle strategy practice had gone well. Nora and Kerr were to be on the sidelines because they didn't have any active abilities to fight in close combat. After they were filled in on their expectations, they took off to the Book Nook to pack up more of the books Kerr wanted to add to the library at his new home.

The Evolved

"Whitley, don't forget to focus! You're not listening to me!" Tahlia called from the sidelines.

Dorian chuckled as Whitley rolled her eyes. Thatcher stood in front of Whitley, bracing himself for what was coming. Whitley crouched down to the ground and took off toward Thatcher at a sprint. Dorian leaned forward, keeping his eyes on Whitley as she dove at Thatcher. In an instant, Whitley was on the other side of Thatcher. She was getting better every day.

"Now, let's make things interesting!" Thatcher yelled as he turned to face Whitley once again. A playful grin played across his face as he threw up a wall of fire in front of him.

Hadley and Tahlia exchanged a knowing look and took a few steps back. Whitley dusted off her jacket and prepared to pounce. Dorian hadn't seen them try this maneuver before, so he rose to his feet to get a better view.

"Oh, please, Thatcher! Don't make me laugh," Whitley shouted just as she leapt at him.

Dorian was amazed to see the wall of fire split open to allow room for Whitley to burst through and knock into Thatcher. Hadley and Tahlia laughed loudly as Thatcher shoved Whitley off him and stood up.

"You weren't supposed to knock me over!" Thatcher said, sounding annoyed.

"That's what you get for being a smartass!" Whitley said between fits of giggles.

"Whitley!" Tahlia scolded.

"Sorry, mom," Whitley said through her giggles.

Dorian laughed and ran up to the group. "That was amazing! You've come a long way, Whitley."

He was greeted by smiles and laughter from the group. "That was brilliant! That will be an incredible defense against Absalom when the day comes. Thatcher, you're able to project a lot more firepower these days. How far do you think you can throw it?" he asked excitedly.

"I don't know, I haven't really tried to throw it, I've mostly used it as a shield for us or tossed a few fireballs for target practice," Thatcher replied, deep in thought.

"Well, what are we waiting for?" Hadley asked, nudging Thatcher playfully.

Dorian watched as Thatcher jogged to the center of the grounds. Thatcher took a deep breath, then stopped, looked at Dorian, and nodded solemnly. He crouched close to the ground and placed his hand flat on the earth. Dorian saw the subtle change in the way Thatcher held himself as the heat began to flow through him. He glanced at Hadley as the sky darkened overhead, and a chill filled the air. She was nervous. Turning his attention back to Thatcher, Dorian studied the way he seemed to let the heat build within him until it reached its highest peak. A single bead of sweat ran down his face. The moment of release sent a solid wall of fire shooting out from Thatcher in all directions.

The next few moments were hectic as Dorian realized the wall of fire was coming straight for them. Whitley let out a small scream as Dorian tried to pull her to safety, and Tahlia called out to Hadley, who stood frozen as the blaze rushed toward her.

The wall of fire was only feet from Hadley, and she hadn't moved. Dorian tried in vain to call out to her. Thatcher came crashing through the fire and attempted to save Hadley. As soon as he touched her, the wind started.

Dorian, Tahlia, and Whitley watched in awe as the wind intensified and swept the fire into a blazing tornado that circled Hadley and Thatcher in a deadly dance. The roar was deafening, and the heat was intense. Then, as quickly as it began, it ended in a downpour of torrential rain.

"Let's get inside!" Tahlia shouted over the rain.

Dorian reluctantly followed Tahlia and Whitley as they took off for the house. Once inside, he glanced back out the large glass doors and could barely make out the embracing figures of Hadley and Thatcher as they shared a kiss.

"That was an interesting development," Whitley said through chattering teeth.

Dorian and Tahlia exchanged a glance, and he knew she understood his thoughts. For the first time since gathering the Evolved, they had made a discovery about what happens when powers are combined.

Chapter Twenty-Eight:
Kerr

Kerr smiled to himself as he stocked the shelves at the book store. Nora was snuggled up on the couch, reading a book about Greek mythology. She had drifted off and was mumbling in her sleep. Ever since she started helping him at the Book Nook, she'd been on a quest to read more about the "mortal" view of the Old Immortals. Every day, they sat huddled around the coffee table with books strewn around them as they fervently took notes and discussed the various legends surrounding their ancestors.

Kerr continued to stock the shelves but stopped when he heard something he'd been waiting for. He climbed down the ladder and quietly sat on the floor next to Nora. Her breathing steadied, and she was still again. Disappointed, Kerr rose to his knees and began to neaten up the books on the table, when she said it again. It was just his name, but it was the most beautiful thing he'd ever heard when it came from her lips. He wasn't sure if he dared to touch her, but curiosity won out. He reached his hand up and gently ran a finger along her cheek and jaw. She smiled in her sleep and uttered his name one more time.

He smiled as his heart skipped a beat, and decided to finish cleaning up. He glanced outside and saw it was still pouring rain. When he finished stacking the books neatly, he heard a small giggle. He turned around to see Nora smiling at him from her spot on the couch.

"What's so funny?" he asked.

"You," she said simply.

Kerr felt hot as they looked into each other's eyes for a few moments. He knew she wasn't looking at him the way he was looking at her, so he turned away hurriedly.

"Well, at least I don't talk in my sleep," Kerr teased.

"Neither do I," Nora replied in embarrassment.

Nora got up and started helping with the daily closing routine. Kerr loved how in sync they were without having to say anything to each other. He handed her the broom, and she tossed him the window cleaner. He was halfway through cleaning the front window when he noticed an instant change in the atmosphere; it got cold and eerily quiet, despite the heavy rain. He tried to peer through the window but stepped back as the frost crept across the glass.

"Um, Nora?" Kerr said nervously as he backed away from the front of the store.

"Shhh!" Nora grabbed him from behind. "Silas."

Kerr threw caution to the wind and pulled her close to him. "What should we do?"

"You need to hide. Now," she replied breathlessly.

"Don't think for one minute I'm going to hide while

you go out and kick some butt," Kerr said indignantly.

Nora thought for a moment, then pouted. "If you're not going to let me play, we're going home."

"Nora, be serious, would you?" Kerr said exasperatedly.

When Nora didn't answer him, he turned around to find her gone. Had she really just left him here? No, Kerr knew better. Nora had gone outside. He knew she could handle herself, but he didn't like the idea of her taking on Silas by herself. Because he didn't see her leave the front of the shop, he turned and made his way through the back room. He found the back door slightly ajar and cautiously peered into the alley. He caught sight of Nora as she lost her footing on the ice and fell hard on her side.

"Are you okay?" he asked quietly as he came up behind her and helped her to her feet.

Nora shook her head. She held her arm up to indicate the injury she'd just sustained. Kerr could sense her pain. He knew the arm was broken, but not just from her aura. The ugly bruise and odd protrusion were evidence enough.

"Okay, Nora, time to stop playing the hero. Let's get you to the E.R." Kerr said.

Nora groaned and rolled her eyes at him. Luckily they hadn't run into Silas out here in the open. Kerr glanced around nervously as he wrapped his arm around Nora's waist and began leading her to the back door.

The Evolved

"Kerr, it really isn't that big of a deal," she said defiantly.

"Really? Okay, open the door. With that arm," Kerr replied evilly.

Nora furrowed her eyebrows and reached for the door. Kerr couldn't believe she was stubborn enough to try it. As she tried to grasp the door handle, she gasped in pain. Kerr reached out to stop her, gently touching her arm in the process. When he did, she gave him a confused look and pulled back in surprise.

"What?" Kerr asked uncomfortably as he ushered her in the back door of the book store.

"Try that again. Touch my arm," Nora instructed.

Kerr looked at her with uncertainty, but reached out and put her arm between his hands. He felt her skin and the sickening lump of broken bone under his hand. She winced but stayed where she was. Kerr didn't know what was supposed to be happening. He mostly just wanted to get her out of there so she could get this bone set. Nora cried out, and Kerr looked from her shocked face to his hands. A green light was coming from his hands, and Kerr could feel her pain lessening. She cried out again as he heard the bone snap back in to place. When the light dissipated, he pulled his hands away. Her arm was perfect, just as it had been before.

"Did I just do that?" Kerr asked in shock.

"Yes," Nora whispered as she dried her cheeks. He hadn't noticed her tears before.

Kerr was still in a state of shock when Nora reached over and took his hand. He felt the room spinning and found himself standing in the middle of Nora's bedroom. Now that they were safe, she seemed to have something else on her mind.

"What did I say?" Nora asked.

"Hmm?" Kerr was still reeling from what happened in the backroom of his book store.

"In my sleep. At the Book Nook, you said I was talking in my sleep," she said quietly.

Kerr hesitated; he didn't want to embarrass her. He wasn't sure how she would react, but he knew she was relentless and would get the answer out of him at some point. He sighed and decided to tell her.

"You said my name," Kerr whispered.

Nora looked up at him. "Oh."

He closed his eyes for a moment, then led her to the bed and gently pushed her down by her shoulders. She looked confused, but sat on the bed and looked up. "Look, Nora, it's okay. I didn't think anything crazy, I just figured you were dreaming about me telling you to put your books away or something. You don't have to freak out. I should probably go tell the others what just happened." Kerr turned to leave the room but was stopped by Nora, grabbing his hand.

"Kerr, I'm sorry. Don't be upset, I just don't know what to say," Nora said, her voice strained.

He looked at her briefly, unsure of what to do. "You don't have to say anything."

The Evolved

She let go of his hand, and he headed for the door. He turned around, wanting to say something to alleviate the awkward direction this conversation had taken. When he turned around, Nora was standing right in front of him.

She reached up and touched his face, then traced her finger along his cheek and jaw, just as he had done to her as she slept. Kerr reached forward and placed his hand on her waist, then pulled her to him gently. He had wanted this moment since he received his prophecy and saw all that could be, and he was going to savor it. He ran his hands slowly up her waist, to her shoulders, then neck, and finally held her face in his hands. Kerr leaned down and slowly traced his lips from her forehead, along her jawline, and finally gave her a gentle, lingering kiss on the lips. As the kiss came to an end, Kerr breathed a sigh of relief.

"Kerr?" Nora asked breathlessly.

"Nora," he responded certainly.

"That is why I was saying your name in my sleep," Nora explained.

Kerr began kissing her again. This time with more passion, as though he were trying to pour his heart and soul into the kiss. She responded, hesitantly at first, then matching his level of intensity. When they pulled away again, Nora gave him a wide smile.

"Why, Kerr Mason! Bless my soul!" Nora said in her best southern accent. She batted her eyes, fanning herself.

Kerr laughed at her. It felt so good to finally break

through the friend zone, and she seemed pleased by what had happened. Without thinking about it, he said what was in his heart.

"You are my future," Kerr told Nora quietly. He waited for her reaction, and when he saw she was simply surprised, he continued, "When I was given my prophecy, I saw you. I saw us. I didn't know what to do. I loved you, and we'd barely spoken to each other. Romulus and Dorian told me to give it time, to get to know you and remember that my visions tell what could be, not what will be. The more time we spend together, the more I want to know about you and want my visions to come true."

"You love me?" Nora whispered.

"Yes," Kerr responded simply.

"Oh," Nora replied.

Nora was quiet for a long time, and Kerr knew he screwed up; he shouldn't have told her. He was starting to freak out when she wrapped her arms around him and buried her face in his chest.

"Kerr, I've never been close to anyone, aside from the Old Immortals. When all the Evolved arrived at our house, I was so surprised to feel so connected with so many more people. When I got my prophecy, I was angry. I don't know what it means, and it's so cryptic; it's frustrating. But the more time I've spent with you, the more I've realized it doesn't have to make sense right now. All that I know right now is that you've become my best friend and more. What I'm trying to say is, I think I love you too," Nora said in a small voice.

The Evolved

He thought his heart was going to burst from his chest as he pulled her body against his. They began kissing eagerly and clinging to one another. Telling the others could wait.

Chapter Twenty-Nine:
Nora

Nora walked out of the bathroom, still wrapped in a towel, and looked at Kerr lying in her bed. She was in a delicious state of disbelief. For some reason, this beautiful man was in love with her. Kerr was propped up on one arm smiling like an idiot.

Nora couldn't help but feel like the luckiest girl in the world. She bounded over to the bed and wrapped her arms around his neck. He laughed at her and kissed her lightly.

"I'm going to like doing that whenever I want," he told her.

"Oh, me too," Nora replied. She kissed his jawline and smiled as he wrapped his arms around her. She wiggled free and jumped off the bed. "I need to get dressed."

She grabbed her clothes and briefly considered dressing in front of him. She decided that would be counterproductive and went into the bathroom. Nora loved the smile on his face and felt satisfied that she had been responsible.

Despite her elation, she didn't know what to say to him after everything they shared. She had never even had a boyfriend before, so she was starting to feel panic welling up from her belly. She felt strange having been so intimate with Kerr so quickly after sharing her feelings. But it felt right, and she thought he felt the same. But what if he didn't? She cleared her throat and reached up to pull her hair back into a messy bun.

As she came out of the bathroom in her jeans and black t-shirt, she decided to take a chance and talk about it.

"So, Kerr, what you said before? About loving me?" Nora's voice broke off at the end, afraid of what he would say.

"Nora, I meant everything I said. I love you. I never would have . . . We never would have . . . I think you know what I mean," he said with a little exasperation.

"Oh good," she said with a smile.

Kerr laughed and went to take a quick shower. Nora decided to exercise her ability a little and focused on Kerr's room. She opened her eyes and found herself staring at the bookshelf in his room. Nora grabbed one of his long-sleeved polo shirts and a pair of jeans. Before she left, she reached in his underwear drawer, blushing slightly as she grabbed the essentials. Closing her eyes, she took herself back to her own room. When her eyes opened, Kerr was standing there in her room with a grin on his face. He thanked her and took the clothes out of her arms.

As soon as Kerr was dressed, they decided to go tell everyone what had happened at the Book Nook. Not only did Silas make his presence known, but Kerr's ability advanced. They had returned to the house with plenty of daylight, but by the time they made their way downstairs, it was well after dinner. They found everyone in the library talking about something that happened with Thatcher and Hadley.

"I hate to interrupt, but we have some news," Nora said as they entered the room. She and Kerr took turns telling their story. When they finished, everyone was silent.

"You are lucky. Silas and Absalom have gotten braver. They've never done anything that could draw attention to themselves before," Dorian said with a worried glance at the floor. "Luckily, the people of Benton are chalking it up to an early winter storm. That's the beauty of the Midwest—lots of unexpected weather."

Nora could tell that Dorian was distraught. She was his only living descendant. If she died, he would live forever with the knowledge of everything he'd lost. She reached over and touched his arm.

"Hey, Dorian, I'm okay. We're okay," she said quietly.

Dorian nodded, then pulled her into a fatherly hug. He kissed the top of her head and tried to hide the tears in his eyes as he turned to Kerr.

"So, you're a healer now?" Thatcher asked with a grin.

Kerr shrugged his shoulders. "I don't know. It was weird. I was thinking about how much I wanted to take her pain away, and then the green light showed up."

The Evolved

Romulus nodded his head. "He isn't a healer necessarily. But from what you told us, it appears he can sense an emotion or feeling, and help correct whatever is causing it. Impressive, son, I can't do that."

"I'm just glad we didn't have to go to the hospital," Nora said, moving over to sit with Kerr. There wasn't room for both of them in the chair, so she climbed on his lap and leaned her head on his shoulder. She blushed slightly when he wrapped his arms around her waist.

Dorian raised his eyebrows at her, and she rolled her eyes at him. Hadley, Whitley, and Tahlia exchanged a grin. Romulus smiled widely, and Thatcher clapped a hand on Kerr's shoulder. Apparently, Nora had been the only one who didn't see how much she and Kerr loved each other.

Hadley and Thatcher began filling them in on what happened at training. Nora felt a twinge of jealousy that she wasn't here to witness their joined powers. All the advances and power bursts they were seeing were indicative of the strength needed for the coming battle.

The rest of the crew went on to explain what had happened here when Silas began his freeze. They received a call from one of the scouts, alerting them to his appearance. They were ready for a fight in case he had the guts to confront them on their turf. It took a few hours to hear back from the scout that there was no sign of him. Apparently, his visit was meant to be a warning to the Evolved.

From her spot on Kerr's lap, she saw Romulus wink at

Kerr. He had already congratulated them on their "joined auras," although she wasn't sure how to take that sentiment. She knew he was happy they had found each other, but she saw a twinge of sorrow when he looked at them. She would give anything to reunite him with Anu, if only it were possible.

Dorian paced back and forth until everyone was seated, then he approached them, holding the Book of Prophecies. He looked frustrated and confused. She'd never seen him at a loss for words. When he finally spoke, it was as though the air left the room.

"It's time."

Romulus was on his feet in a moment, and Tahlia gasped loudly.

"It's time for us to take the fight to them. It's time for us to take the next step toward bringing in the New Era," Dorian said quietly.

"What do we need to do?" Whitley asked with a shiver.

Dorian closed his eyes and stared at the book. "I don't know."

Three simple words that left everyone feeling lost.

"What do you mean you don't know?" Kerr demanded.

"The book doesn't tell us everything. In fact, the book only has our history and your prophecies. The Creator was always adamant that nothing could be pre-written, that you have the will to choose what happens after your prophecies," Romulus told them.

Nora felt Kerr hold her closer. She knew he had figured

out that his prophecy had to do with embracing the future, and that she was part of it. But how would that help them in a battle against Silas and Absalom? She still didn't know what her prophecy meant, but she gathered that she would play an integral part in ushering in the New Era.

"We won't be rushing into anything this moment, but we need to begin formulating a plan," Tahlia said. "They need more training," she told Dorian imploringly.

Dorian nodded his head. "You're right. We will prepare, and we will end this at the Winter Solstice."

* * *

It had been over a month since they met in the library. Every day had been filled with more training and more battle strategy. Nora was exhausted. She had pushed herself to use her ability to its fullest extent, and it had taken a lot out of her. Her fellow Evolved were also feeling the strain. They were all appreciative that Tahlia insisted that they have a break from training to enjoy a family Thanksgiving celebration. Although they refused to accept that they were partially relieved because it could be their last chance to celebrate together. The Winter Solstice was now less than a month away, and they were facing the hard reality that they may not all make it to Christmas.

Nora was lying in bed with Kerr, enjoying the smell of the pies baking in the oven. She kissed his cheek and snuggled in as he tightened his grip on her. They were both exhausted. She sighed loudly and let the rhythm of Kerr's heart lull her to sleep.

She looked at the ceiling in the room. She heard the steady beep of the heart rate monitor. She grimaced as the pain started to spread across her abdomen again. Looking to the side, she saw the numbers on the monitor rise higher and higher as the pain intensified. Where was Kerr? A nurse came in and told her it was time to push. Kerr rushed to her side with an apologetic shrug. He took her hand, bringing it to his lips for a firm kiss. She noticed their matching wedding bands and smiled weakly. The nurse asked if she was ready, and she nodded her head. Squeezing Kerr's hand, she began to push.

"Gah!" Nora said loudly and woke with a start. She couldn't help herself, she reached over and shoved Kerr.

"Ugh, what was that for?" Kerr yelled.

"You should know!" Nora yelled back.

Kerr looked at her like she'd lost her mind and shook his head.

"Like maybe you could have told me we're going to get married? Or that we're going to have a kid? That was not just a dream. I felt it all. I felt the contractions, I felt you holding my hand, and I felt myself pushing out a freakin' baby!" she said seething.

Kerr looked at her closely. She knew he was trying to read her. Her irritation turned to alarm when his eyes grew wide in disbelief.

"Kerr? What is it?" she asked with concern as her panic level began to rise.

The Evolved

"How did you see that?" Kerr asked.

"Yeah, I am not the one answering questions right now. Spit. It. Out," Nora said, enunciating each word.

"You know how I told you I saw a lot about our future when I received my prophecy?" he asked slowly. When Nora nodded, he continued, "Well, what I didn't tell you, or anyone is that I also know roughly what all of our prophecies mean."

"Are you kidding me? You've known all this time, and you haven't shared? You've seen the frustration everyone is feeling with their prophecies, and you didn't think it was time to tell us?" Nora was shouting by the time she finished. "I think I'm going to be sick."

Nora got up and ran for the bathroom. She was heaving her guts out when she realized Kerr had entered the bathroom with her. She groaned as he began rubbing her back and holding her hair out of her face. When she finally finished, he handed her a glass of water and had her toothbrush ready. She was still livid with him and began brushing her teeth while glaring at him.

"I couldn't tell anyone. I can't now either. Like Romulus said, the rest of our story couldn't be written in the Book of Prophecies because we had the ability to choose," he pleaded with her as she wiped the toothpaste off her face.

She reached for the doorknob, but Kerr stopped her. "You might want to be in here when I tell you what I know."

She eyed him suspiciously and perched on the edge of

the tub. When she didn't say anything, he must have decided to get on with the story. He sighed and sat down next to her.

"Well, what you saw was a vision I had of you while we were sleeping. I didn't know you could see it too. Long story short? You're pregnant."

"WHAT?!" Nora shouted. "How could I possibly be . . . Oh my gosh, are you freakin' kidding me? You better tell me everything you saw that involves me."

"In a nutshell? I saw us falling in love, which already happened. We're going to get married, and we're going to have a baby," Kerr said.

"Well, clearly, we missed a step. Is that where the whole free will part comes into play?" Nora asked rhetorically.

Kerr sat quietly while she ranted for a few more minutes, then he caught her attention by getting down on his knees.

"I'm sorry, Nora. I should have told you." The way he hung his head, she could tell he thought she was mad. She didn't really know what she was feeling. How could she be mad at him when he wasn't in this alone? Nora got down on her knees and lifted his face, so they were nose to nose.

"This is not your fault. This was meant to be. I finally understand my prophecy. It's the baby, isn't it? The future will come from within me? This baby is part of the Creators plan," Nora said as she began to cry. Kerr nodded solemnly at her before pulling her into a tight hug.

The Evolved

"I love you, Nora Lowell," he said through his own tears.

"And I love you, Kerr Mason," she said, and she kissed him deeply.

Chapter Thirty:
Whitley

Whitley had not been with her mother for a holiday since she was little. Tahlia took on the task of preparing the Thanksgiving dinner, and Whitley readily volunteered to assist. They finished the pies and left them cooling as they began the prep work for the morning.

"I can't believe dad agreed to come tomorrow," Whitley said to her mother.

"I know. I'm nervous. Is that silly?" Tahlia sounded like a teenage girl.

"It's not silly, mom. There are a lot of unresolved feelings between you two, and you've been talking a lot more lately," Whitley replied. She secretly hoped her parents could rekindle their romance, but it seemed unlikely.

Whitley worked on the island in the kitchen while her mother was doing dishes. From the kitchen window, they could see Hadley practicing her ability with Dorian. She was now able to not only control the weather but also conjure it in her hands. As a result, she was throwing lightning bolts at a tree in the backyard. Whitley smiled as she thought about how far they'd come. Thatcher had been partnering with

The Evolved

Hadley to perfect their fire tornado and had also found a way to make fire fall from the sky like rain. Whitley had been working with Tahlia and learned how to use her ability as a sort of telekinesis. She could manipulate matter and channel energy. She felt stronger every day, but she also felt insecure.

Kerr and Nora weren't much help in battle because they had what Tahlia referred to as passive powers. They were using them in practice by assuming they would be on the sidelines and used as a distraction. Kerr was advancing faster than anyone. He learned how to focus his ability in order to anticipate an opponent's next move in battle, and was working on projecting his healing ability from a distance. Nora was practicing communicating with the Evolved through telepathy and could now transport them at a moment's notice without the dizziness and nausea. They decided that Romulus would guard Kerr and Nora, while Tahlia would join the Evolved in battle. Dorian would be the decoy to draw Silas and Absalom to them.

The battle plans had been made, and now they were just waiting. No one had heard from Malcolm, and the scouts hadn't spotted him again since he disappeared. He was still an unknown in the scheme of battle, but Thatcher was searching for him tirelessly.

Tahlia finished loading the dishwasher and turned to face Whitley.

"Done?" she asked.

Whitley nodded and headed to wash her hands as Tahlia put the chopped vegetables in the fridge.

"This all feels so . . . normal," Whitley said as she dried her hands.

"I know, honey," Tahlia said sadly. "I won't tell you everything will be alright because I don't know that."

Whitley hugged her mother and linked arms with her as they left the kitchen. The kitchen opened into the entryway, which held the stairs leading to the bedrooms. Whitley looked up and saw Kerr and Nora coming down the stairs hand in hand. They complimented each other so well that it didn't surprise anyone when they finally got together. Whitley felt a pang of jealousy that the other Evolved had managed to couple off and shared a deeper connection than she would ever feel with any of them. But she had the opportunity to spend more time with her mother, and that had meant more to her than any romantic relationship could.

"Hey, Nora, how was your nap?" Whitley asked suggestively. She was the one to suggest that Nora rest. Whitley was actually a little irritated that Kerr seemed to have infiltrated her nap time. Nora had been so tired and out of it lately that Whitley thought she would benefit from a rest. It was all she could do to convince her to let Tahlia and Whitley handle the Thanksgiving preparations.

"Too short," Nora replied. Whitley noticed how pale she was, which only cemented her worry.

"You don't have to get up if you're still tired. Perhaps I should take Kerr into town for coffee so you can actually get some rest," Whitley said pointedly.

"Oh no, it wasn't anything like that." Nora giggled.

The Evolved

"Where is everyone?"

"Hadley and Dorian are outside. Thatcher is playing a video game with Romulus in the basement. Eric is on his way, he should be here any minute," Tahlia replied. "Why? What's up?"

"We just have something we want to discuss with everyone before tomorrow. My parents don't really know about all of this," Kerr replied hurriedly.

"Okay, I'll grab the guys. Mom can get Dorian and Hadley," Whitley replied.

Soon everyone was gathered around the dining room table. Nora and Kerr stood at the head of the table. Whitley had a feeling this was going to be some cheesy engagement announcement or a sentimental pre-Thanksgiving speech.

"Now that we have everyone together, there are few things we need to discuss," Nora said with a business-like tone. "We've all been working so hard to learn about our abilities and come up with a game plan, that time has passed without us even realizing it."

Yep, sentimental pre-Thanksgiving speech. Whitley put her elbow on the oak table and rested her head on her hand.

"Like the rest of you, I've spent a significant amount of time thinking about my prophecy." Nora continued, "Today, I have finally figured out what my prophecy will mean for me."

Whitley noticed that Romulus was deliberately not looking at Kerr or Nora. She assumed it was because he wanted them to be able to say whatever they needed to, rather than read it in their minds. She could tell how difficult it seemed to be for him because he was unusually jittery.

"I'm sure my prophecy is not as fresh in your minds as it is in mine, but I was told not to think of myself as being part of the end because the beginning would come from within me." Nora placed her hand over her stomach, and realization began to dawn in Whitley's mind.

"Shut up!" Hadley squealed.

Romulus was up and bear-hugging Nora and Kerr in a heartbeat. Tahlia was bouncing in her seat. Thatcher looked confused, but Dorian was unreadable. He looked almost angry as he took in this information. Whitley made her way up to Nora and held her closely.

"Well, I guess that explains a lot," she whispered in Nora's ear.

Nora smiled when she pulled away. Whitley felt almost giddy for the first time in months. One of the group had figured out their purpose! Soon everyone had hugged Nora and Kerr except for Dorian. It was very out of character for him to not show affection to Nora, especially when she was happy or excited.

Whitley grabbed Hadley's hand and pulled her out of the way. Tahlia was behind Thatcher with her hand on one of his shoulders, as if to hold him back. Romulus had one hand on Kerr's shoulder and the other hand on Nora's shoulder. Nora looked expectantly at Dorian as he approached. He stopped directly in front of Nora and took both her hands in his. Whitley could now see the tears in his eyes, but she was still unsure of what they meant. The tension was palpable as they waited for him to speak.

"You are no longer my final descendant," Dorian said in a curious tone. "I will not die when you claim all your power."

Nora bit her lip as she nodded her head slowly as tears ran down her cheeks. Whitley choked back tears of her own as she watched the scene unfold.

"I feel like this child has given me my life back, but I know this will also put you in more danger," Dorian said, looking troubled. "I had not been prepared for this."

"It will change nothing, brother," Romulus reassured him. "Nora was never going to be an active part of our fight. I will watch out for her."

Dorian was about to reply when the doorbell rang.

"Saved by the bell!" Thatcher cheered as he headed for the door. Whitley had the feeling all the emotions and family togetherness was making him uncomfortable.

Whitley squeezed Hadley's hand as they waited for their father to enter the room. But the last person they expected to see was Malcolm.

Chapter Thirty-One:
Thatcher

Thatcher opened the door to find a man holding the lifeless body of Malcolm. He was dumbfounded. When he opened the door, he was expecting to greet the future President of the United States but was instead faced with a bleeding and bruised thirteen-year-old boy. The man introduced himself as Ross, one of Eric Callaghan's private guards. He explained that they had been doing a perimeter check before allowing Mr. Callaghan to enter.

"The kid was just lying in the road right before we got to the driveway. When I got out of the car to investigate, he was barely conscious. He kept saying Thatcher and asking for help. I picked him up and ran," Ross explained. "We need to complete our perimeter check."

Thatcher took the boy from his arms and rushed him into the rest of the group. As soon as he set Malcolm down, he motioned for Hadley and Whitley to follow him. Dorian was close behind.

"We need to check the grounds. I don't know what happened to him or how he got here, but we need to make sure he came alone," Thatcher told the twins.

"You need to make sure those security guards are not

put in harm's way. They are no match for Absalom and Silas," Dorian told them urgently.

They nodded at him and went outside.

The three split up to make sure Malcolm had arrived alone. Thatcher took the unlit wooded area that separated the house from the road. Hadley went to the right and would head to the back of the house, meeting her twin, who took the opposite route. It was imperative that he move quietly for fear of encountering Silas or Absalom. He sent a small fireball ahead of him to light the way; it wouldn't do him any favors to meet someone in the dark. The fireball split in two and floated along in front of him on either side of his body. He walked through the trees like this for a few minutes before deciding it would take too long to search this way. As soon as he thought it, the fireball burst into the sky like fireworks suspended in air. The woods were instantly illuminated with a dull light. The trees around him were now well-lit, and he saw that they were quiet and empty of any threats. He made his way to the road and found only staggering footprints in the dirt road. It appeared that Malcolm had approached the house on foot, which brought more worry than comfort to Thatcher.

He looked around for a few more minutes, then headed back to the house. The twins were waiting for him at the front door. They shook their heads to tell him they found nothing. Thatcher nodded and told them what he found.

When the three of them returned to the dining room, they saw Tahlia and Dorian busying themselves over

Malcolm. They had stripped him down to his boxers to get a better look at his injuries. Romulus had his hands on Malcolm's temples in an effort to determine what happened to him. Kerr returned with clean towels, rubbing alcohol, and antibiotic cream.

"Kerr, can you do your weird healing thing?" Whitley whispered to him.

"I tried. He's not conscious. I can't sense his feelings. If I can't sense his feelings, I can't help him," Kerr said sadly.

Tahlia began cleaning the wounds, muttering to herself about the severity of some of them. She looked at Thatcher briefly with a sad look in her eyes, then continued with her work.

"What can I do?" Thatcher asked desperately as he took in the broken body of the young boy in front of him.

"I'm going to need you to cauterize these wounds," Tahlia said seriously.

"What? No. No way." Thatcher felt his stomach start to turn.

"Thatcher, it would take too long to get him to a hospital or call an ambulance to come here. My only other option is to heat a knife, but if he moves, I could cut him. Focus. You can do it," Tahlia told him sternly.

Thatcher looked at Hadley, who offered him a supportive nod. After that, they fell into a rhythm of cleaning and cauterizing. Once all the wounds were closed, Dorian helped apply the antibiotic cream and dress the wounds.

Just as they were finishing, the doorbell rang again. This time, Thatcher, Hadley, and Whitley went to the door. They exchanged a grave look before Thatcher reached forward and pulled it open.

"Daddy!" the twins squealed in unison.

His security detail had finished their perimeter check and deemed the house safe enough for Eric to enter. Good thing there weren't any paparazzi around to capture this moment.

"Are your security guards coming in?" Thatcher asked as he glanced outside.

"No. They only came to check the location. I insisted on being free to spend this time with my family and sent them home to theirs," Eric replied.

Thatcher nodded his head. "It's nice to meet you, sir, but I need to get back to the other room."

Thatcher shut the large front door and went back to Malcolm.

Romulus was having a hushed discussion with Dorian, as Tahlia lovingly wiped the dirt and blood from the rest of his body.

"He lost a lot of blood, Thatcher. These wounds were deep, but they weren't done with any manmade object. Romulus was pretty shaken when he finished reading him. Only time will tell if he will recover. I will put him on a blow-up bed in my room until he improves." Tahlia looked stricken at the state of this boy.

Romulus helped take Malcolm upstairs while Kerr and Tahlia got the bed ready. Tahlia took the time to clean up, so she didn't greet her ex-husband while covered in blood.

Once Malcolm was situated, Kerr went to check on Nora. Tahlia made her way downstairs to be with her family. Thatcher stayed next to Malcolm until Romulus and Dorian joined him to tell him what they knew.

"He was tortured," Dorian told Thatcher.

"That son of a . . . "

"Thatcher!" Romulus chided.

"What did they do to him?" Thatcher spat as the anger burned in his chest.

"Absalom had been punishing him for leaving us. His purpose was to infiltrate the Evolved and undermine our plans. Instead, he left and went back to the one person he thought supported him." Romulus continued, "When Absalom tired of burning him, Silas threw ice shards at him. They were going to kill him when Malcolm had a burst of power. His pain, anger, and hurt all boiled over, and he burst through the roof of the metal building Absalom called his lair and flew away. He made it to Benton and collapsed."

Thatcher was shaking his head, thinking about the pain and betrayal Malcolm must have felt when he discovered he truly was just a pawn in their game.

"He's just a kid. He didn't deserve this. It would have been better if Absalom had just killed him like he did the rest of the descendants of the Old Immortals,"

The Evolved

Thatcher said bitterly. "He's just a kid."

He knew the last statement sounded more like a plea than a statement, but he didn't know how to process what had happened to Malcolm. The kid was raised in hate, conditioned to believe the worst of the people who were destined to destroy those who had spared him. His parents were murdered by Absalom and Silas, but they raised him to believe they had to die. He couldn't handle the possibility that Malcolm would never wake up from this.

"What do we do now?" Thatcher asked quietly.

"Nothing. We continue with our plan. Absalom and Silas knew that Malcolm would come to us. They would have stopped him if they wanted to. They were counting on him being the catalyst to provoke us before we were prepared to attack," Dorian told Thatcher firmly.

"We do nothing?" Thatcher responded enraged.

Both Dorian and Romulus nodded at him solemnly. "The anger you feel right now isn't going to go away. It will continue to build, and you will be able to gain restitution for what was done to Malcolm. We just ask that you stay the course."

Thatcher was angry at first, and couldn't bring himself to even look at either of them. He finally closed his eyes against his tears of frustration and nodded his head.

"Alright. I see your point. Right now, I just want him to be okay. I will do everything I can to help him make a full recovery so he can be there when we finally stop

Absalom and Silas."

"There's more, Thatcher," Romulus said, giving Dorian a sideways look. "Absalom is Malcolm's father."

"What? How?" Thatcher was completely stricken.

"I'll let Malcolm tell you the details when he wakes, but that's why he was tortured. Absalom told him when he returned, and Malcolm told him you were right and refused to help him," Romulus said.

Thatcher stared at Malcolm lying lifelessly on the blow-up bed. His breathing was steady. Aside from the freshly-cauterized scars and burn marks, he looked as though he was simply sleeping. Thatcher's chest hurt just thinking about everything Malcolm had endured because he stood up for what was right.

Chapter Thirty-Two:
Hadley

Hadley woke up on Thanksgiving morning to the sound of pans clanging in the kitchen. She stretched and climbed out of bed. She looked at the clock and realized the sun hadn't risen yet. Turning back to her bed, she briefly considered climbing back in, but the idea of joining her mother and sister in the kitchen was far too attractive. The walls in her room were painted a misty gray with a bold yellow pattern swirling all over. She had really come to appreciate the accents throughout the house. Everything seemed so perfectly planned. Hadley made her bed, smoothing out the duvet cover with its embroidered birds and branches.

She went to the attached bathroom and quickly undressed to get in the shower. Once she had finished brushing through her hair, she picked out an indigo sweater dress and gray leggings. As soon as she was ready, she bounded down the stairs.

Hadley was surprised to find her father helping her mother instead of Whitley. It warmed her heart to see them getting along so well. In fact, they seemed to be more than just getting along.

"Morning, sweetheart!" her father sang out as he

rounded the island to give her a hug.

"Hey, guys, what can I help with?" Hadley asked.

"You could tear the bread for the stuffing," her mother responded.

Hadley went over to the bread, then started pulling it into small chunks and tossing it in the large bowl. She remembered helping her mother with this when she was little. It was one of the few jobs she and Whitley could help with that didn't involve touching something hot or messy.

"Here, Lia," she heard her father say as he handed Tahlia a cup of coffee. "You too, Had?"

Hadley nodded appreciatively as Eric poured another cup and added her favorite creamer. She took a sip of her coffee and smiled at her parents, who were moving around each other effortlessly as they finished preparing the turkey and placing it in the oven.

"How is Malcolm doing, mom?" Hadley asked, afraid to know the answer.

Tahlia looked tired and concerned as she shook her head. "He didn't wake at all, but his sleep doesn't appear restful. He's so pale and broken."

"Thatcher stayed with him last night. He wouldn't leave his side. I let your mother sleep in my room," Eric replied.

Hadley raised her eyebrows pointedly. "I'm sorry, what?"

Tahlia rolled her eyes. "Your father and I are adults. We can sleep together if we want."

"Mom! Yuck! I can't believe we're talking about this," Hadley replied in shock.

"Oh. No. Hadley, that's not what I meant," Tahlia tried to explain. "I meant we slept together. We didn't sleep together."

"Yeah, that clears things up," Hadley said, looking from Eric to Tahlia, who was waiting for an explanation.

Tahlia crossed her arms in front of her, refusing to answer. Eric caught Tahlia's eye and started giggling, which was very uncharacteristic for him. Hadley was completely exasperated by them both, but couldn't help but smile. They were acting like a couple of teenagers, and she was acting like the mom.

"Oh, for cripes' sake," Hadley said, throwing her hands in the air and leaving the kitchen.

Hadley walked down the hall to the library. She hadn't read a good book in a while, and since they had a day off, she might as well enjoy it. She had never gone to Dorian's library just to look for a book, and she really didn't know where to begin. With all the prophecies and destiny stuff, Hadley decided to close her eyes and reach for a book; surely the book she grabbed would mean something.

Opening her eyes, Hadley looked down at the book she was holding. Her stomach clenched as she saw that it was the one Thatcher had told her about, History of the Old Immortals. She decided to apply the same principle to the section she would read. She closed her eyes and thumbed through, then stopped at a random page.

History of the Old Immortals:
Tahlia

According to legend, the first woman brought forth the end of an era. The Old Era saw the Creator walking amongst his creations, teaching, and guiding them in a new world. The Creator gave his people the will to choose their own path, and with that, he gave his first woman a golden sphere. This sphere held all evils and struggles that could befall the world.

Now Absalom had already fallen from grace and spent his days trying to gain the upper hand on the Creator. Absalom went to the first woman, sometimes called Eve or Pandora, and convinced her that the Creator actually wanted the sphere closed because it held power and knowledge he did not want his people to have.

The seed of doubt Absalom had placed in her mind was her undoing. In a fit of jealous rage, the woman threw the sphere to the ground, shattering it and severing the link between the Creator and his creations.

Each tiny piece began to change into the various evils contained within. The first woman cried out in anguish. Believing all hope was lost, she begged the Creator to forgive her. The Creator could not come to her, for she had disobeyed him and released the evil.

After all the pieces had transformed and flown away,

the final piece of the sphere began to vibrate and glow. This final piece transformed into a woman. Tahlia, sometimes called Elpis, was the Creator's gift to his people; she was created to bring hope to a hopeless world.

"What the . . . ?" Hadley was so confused by what she just read. She knew her mother was one of the Virtues. She was hope. But what she just read told her that her mother literally was the embodiment of hope. The more she thought about it, the more it made sense. Everything her mother accomplished had spawned hope. Her mother was the only Old Immortal female to have children, and that gave the others hope that there could still be a future for them. She left her family, hoping it would keep them safe. The fact that she was still out there alive left Hadley with the hope that she would someday find her mother again. And now, as Tahlia busied herself in the kitchen with her estranged husband, she gave their family hope that they could be whole again.

Hadley's head was spinning. There was more to read, but she had to put the book down before she passed out. Her mother had been released from Pandora's Box? Her mother came from the forbidden fruit Eve plucked from the tree of knowledge? But those weren't the real stories, they were variations. Just as Dorian had told them, they are the gods and goddesses of every mythology and every religion.

She put the book back on the shelf and turned to leave the library. Hadley didn't know why she was meant to read that section, but she silently thanked the Creator for the information.

The Evolved

As she entered the kitchen, she was pleased to see more of the family coming down to join the Thanksgiving preparation. Kerr and Whitley were both sipping coffee at the island, and Dorian was putting dishes in the dishwasher.

Hadley signaled to Whitley that she needed to come closer, and waited anxiously as her twin approached. She took Whitley by the hand and led her back to the library.

"Here, read this," Hadley said as she handed the book to her sister.

Whitley gasped as she read and looked up at her sister a few times. When she finally finished, she closed the book and looked at the floor for a few moments.

"How did you find this?" Whitley asked.

"I was bored and looking for something to read. I came in here and just grabbed a book. Remember when we used to do that at the library? Or when we couldn't decide which mystery novel to buy at a book store?" Hadley asked.

Whitley nodded. Her eyes were wide as she looked at her sister. "So, what does that mean? Mom is hope, she's not just the Virtue?"

Hadley shrugged. "I guess. I've sort of given up being surprised by this stuff."

Whitley laughed and agreed. The girls got up and went back out to the kitchen. Whitley grabbed her coffee and offered Hadley a cup, which she readily accepted.

It all seemed so normal. Anyone looking in would

think they were just a large family preparing for their holiday meal. Hadley felt bad about razzing her parents so badly, especially after what she just read. It couldn't be easy for her mother to be the hope of all mankind for millennia. She remembered her mother telling them that being with Eric and having the twins was the only time she had ever been selfish in her life.

She looked around the kitchen, realizing that her mother was missing from the bunch. Tahlia must have gone to check on Malcolm. Hadley realized the sun had risen, and it was now almost eight o'clock. She wondered if Thatcher had slept at all last night. She heard someone coming down the stairs and saw her mother come around the corner.

Tahlia glanced nervously at Hadley. She must have been expecting more questions. But Hadley just smiled apologetically and winked. A slow grin spread across Tahlia's face, and she hugged Hadley tightly. Tahlia went over to the breakfast table where Eric was sitting. She sidled up to him and leaned her head on his shoulder. They looked as though they had finally found peace again. Hadley could get used to having both parents.

Chapter Thirty-Three:
Kerr

Kerr took a deep breath and knocked on the bedroom door. He heard Nora groan from the other side and grinned to himself.

"Nora, it's me, can I come in?" he asked.

"Depends. Are you going to get me pregnant again?" she asked.

Kerr laughed and opened the door. Nora was lying on the bed with the blankets over her head. She peeked out at him and groaned again.

"How ya feelin?" Kerr asked as he sat on the edge of the bed.

"Better. The food smells really good," Nora said quietly.

Kerr smiled at her and leaned down to kiss her forehead. Nora smiled at him as she sat up in bed.

"So, I was thinking . . . " Kerr began.

"This could be dangerous," Nora teased.

"Well, my mom and stepdad are coming for dinner today, and I thought I could introduce you as my future wife," Kerr said hesitantly.

The Evolved

"Wait, what?" Nora asked, taken off guard.

"I would like to introduce you as my future wife," Kerr repeated.

"That's a little quick, don't you think?" Nora questioned.

"Really? I mean, *really*?" Kerr said with a furrowed brow.

Nora thought for a moment as her hand flew to her stomach. Then she laughed. Kerr loved the sound, but he still didn't have an answer.

"Your future wife, huh? Does that mean we're going to tell them about the baby?" Nora asked uncertainly.

Kerr smiled at Nora. "Is that a yes?"

"No," Nora said defiantly.

"Oh," Kerr replied, deflated.

"It's an absolutely," Nora said, lunging at him.

Kerr hugged her close and kissed her as she giggled. Everything was falling into place for them, and he was elated. Kerr pulled away and grinned widely at Nora. It was so surreal how quickly everything in his life had changed, but he wouldn't change a single moment of it.

"You better get up and get ready. It's already almost noon. We're just waiting for the turkey to be done. My family will be here soon," Kerr said.

"Oh gosh, you're already starting to boss me around?" Nora said, throwing her pillow at him.

Kerr dodged the pillow and closed the door behind him. He made his way down the hall and down the stairs. At the base of the stairs, Romulus was waiting for him. He couldn't stop the grin from spreading across his face when he saw his many times' great-grandpa.

"Congratulations, son. I am so proud of you," Romulus said, slapping him on the back.

"Thank you. I think I'm in shock. She actually wants to marry me," Kerr said, then he smiled slyly. "By the way, it's going to be a girl."

Romulus let out a whoop and hugged Kerr. This would be the first girl born to his bloodline. Kerr knew it would mean a lot to him, especially when he found out what her name would be. But Kerr decided to keep that a secret. Nora didn't even know yet. The doorbell rang, and Kerr knew it was time to introduce his mother to his new life. He opened the front door and was surrounded by the hugs of his mother and stepfather.

"How are you, son?" his stepfather asked.

"I'm doing great. I can't wait for you guys to meet everyone," Kerr said warmly.

He loved his stepdad, Andrew, but he never called him dad. His mother remarried shortly before he turned ten, and while Kerr knew this was good for her and could see the happiness surrounding them both, Andrew wasn't Cole. He knew Andrew never tried to take Cole's place, and he always respected the traditions and family heirlooms that kept Kerr's real father alive for Kerr and his mother, Melanie. He still hadn't told them about the Evolved or his own ability. He felt like telling his mother would somehow tarnish his father's memory and lead her to worry about Kerr. Now that he was expecting a child of his own, he needed her to believe he was strong and stable.

"Mom, Andrew, I want you to meet Romulus," Kerr said, gesturing behind him. He winced slightly when his mother stared open-mouthed at Romulus, no doubt recognizing the similarities between him and her late husband.

"Pleasure to meet you, Mr. and Mrs. Hodges," Romulus said with a slight bow. "Kerr has told us so much about you both."

Kerr led them into the dining room where they were greeted by everyone but Nora and Thatcher. He knew Nora would be down soon, but Thatcher would probably remain by Malcolm's side. Once he'd made introductions all the way around, he was pleased to see Nora coming down the stairs.

"Oh, Nora!" he said excitedly. "Mom, Andrew, this is Nora, my fiancé."

He heard a sharp intake of breath from Hadley and Whitley as they attempted not to squeal with delight. Tahlia smiled warmly at them, with Eric at her side. Dorian nodded approvingly. Kerr had already obtained his blessing. His mother had tears in her eyes as she looked at the two of them, and Andrew smiled proudly.

"It's nice to meet you, Melanie and Andrew. You have an amazing son," Nora said shyly.

Kerr was pleased to see his mother rush forward and

gather Nora into her arms.

"I've always wanted a daughter," Kerr heard her whisper.

Nora blushed. Andrew approached her and gave her a tight hug. After the introductions were complete, everyone sat around the large table. Thatcher had not appeared, but no one wanted to draw attention to that while Kerr's parents were visiting. They enjoyed a delicious Thanksgiving meal together, then everyone retired to the sitting room for coffee and tea.

"Tahlia, the meal was delicious," Melanie said politely.

"Thank you. Eric and the girls helped me. It's been a long time since I made a feast for so many people," Tahlia replied warmly.

"We really must be going, dear," Andrew told his wife apologetically. "We promised to make a few other stops this evening, and we don't want you to feel the need to entertain us."

Kerr had expected them to stay a little longer but understood why they would say their goodbyes. He hadn't been forthcoming with the reason why he moved into this house with all these people he had only just met. Kerr decided his mother only came to make sure he was alright. Both she and Andrew seemed satisfied that there was nothing to worry about, so they were ready to take their leave. It was better for them to live in ignorance than to know that Kerr was preparing for a prophesied battle with a group of other people with special abilities. He had a feeling they would have locked him up for that.

The Evolved

He got up and led them to the door, motioning for Nora to follow. Once they were in the foyer, he took Nora's hand and shared the rest of his good news.

"Mom, Nora and I are expecting a baby," Kerr said gently, unsure of how she would react.

His mother was silent for a few moments, as though it was too much to process in one day. She looked at the two of them, assessing the situation as he had seen her do so many times before. Kerr prepared himself for the onslaught of questions he was sure were about to come.

"Okay," she replied. "You're young. You've only known each other for about two months. But I can see that you love each other deeply."

Nora let out a cry of relief. "You have no idea, Melanie. Your son is the most amazing person I have ever met. We have spent a lot of time together, and I know it sounds crazy or naïve, but Kerr is the man for me, and he would be even if it weren't for the baby."

Kerr squeezed her hand and kissed her hair. She smelled amazing, as always, and he couldn't wait to give her everything she ever wanted. His mother smiled at the two of them.

"So, I'm going to be a grandma," she said happily.

"Yes. And Andrew is going to be a grandpa," Kerr said simply. He noticed the sentiment took his stepdad by surprise. He probably hadn't expected that Kerr would encourage his children to call him grandpa. The truth was, Andrew had never been his father; he had known and loved his father with all his heart. But from the day his daughter is born, she will know three men as her grandfather. Andrew, Dorian, and Romulus. What a lucky little girl.

Chapter Thirty-Four:
Malcolm

When he woke up, he looked around the room. At first, he didn't know where he was. He started to panic. Malcolm opened his eyes and saw Thatcher staring at him.

"Hey," Malcolm said weakly.

"Hey, kid," Thatcher replied.

"I'm sorry," Malcolm told him.

"Malcolm, it's alright. You didn't know any better," Thatcher reassured him.

"He's my father. He told me about how much he loved my mother, then he tortured me. How could he do that? How could someone be so awful?" Malcolm asked.

Thatcher just shook his head at him and shrugged.

"He's evil," Thatcher said.

"I know. I guess I've always known. But I thought it was okay. He had convinced me that my parents died because of the Evolved. He had convinced me that the only reason I was alive was because he was protecting me. I know that was a lie, but I still don't know the truth," Malcolm said sadly.

The Evolved

Malcolm kept reliving the last month in his mind. The pain he had endured was more than he could handle. Absalom and Silas made a game out of torturing him. Each time he begged for death, they would leave him to heal so they could start over. He tried to sit up, but the air mattress was making a lot of noise, and he was in a lot of pain.

"Hold on, Malcolm. Let me go get Kerr. He can help you," Thatcher said as he got up to leave the room. "I'll be right back, don't move."

Malcolm lay in the bed, waiting for Thatcher to return. He told him not to move, but Malcolm wasn't sure that he could move on his own anyway. He was trying to keep his emotions under control. He had made some awful decisions in his life, but he couldn't help but feel like some of those decisions were made for him. Absalom raised him for a specific reason; to infiltrate the Evolved and eventually help him take over the world. He choked back a sob and closed his eyes. Now that he knew the truth about why Absalom let him live, he knew he could help the Evolved gain the upper hand. Despite his ruthless behavior, he had a weak spot. Cassandra was his weak spot. He opened his eyes to see Thatcher and Kerr file into the room.

"Kerr's ability has advanced. He can sense pain and heal whatever it is that is causing the pain," Thatcher told him.

"Just my body, though, right?" Malcolm asked apprehensively. When he saw the confusion on Thatcher's face, he continued, "I'm dealing with some emotional pain too, but I need to keep that. I need it to help you."

Kerr stepped forward and smiled at him. "I don't think I can take away emotional pain. But I will make sure to only focus on your physical pain, okay?"

Malcolm nodded his head. He watched Kerr place his hands on Malcolm's abdomen. The pain came to the surface, and Malcolm cried out, but his hurt was soon forgotten as he saw the green light wrap its way around his body. Soon his whole body was glowing, and his pain was intensifying. It felt like every injury was migrating toward the center of his body as the light drew back to Kerr's hands. Malcolm clenched his fists and yelled out in agony as the pain reached its peak, then it suddenly dissipated. Kerr stepped back and sat on a chair in the corner, the look on his face unreadable. Now that the physical pain was gone, the emotional turmoil he was in resurfaced, and Malcolm let out a sob.

"Why?" he asked Thatcher and Kerr imploringly. "Why me? Why did he do this? How could someone be filled with so much hate?"

Kerr gave him a sympathetic shrug. Malcolm could tell he had no answers. He had probably asked those same questions ever since he witnessed Absalom murdering his father. That realization brought on a new wave of sadness. His father had taken away so much from each of the Evolved. He looked up at Kerr and shook his head.

"I am so sorry, Kerr. I'm sure it's hard for you to help me. I'm his son, and he took away your dad," Malcolm said.

The Evolved

"It wasn't your fault, kid. Absalom has been a psycho for a long time. Long before any of us were even thought of," Kerr answered.

Malcolm got up and looked down. The first thing he noticed was that he was covered in large ugly scars. They would serve as constant reminders of the torture he lived through. They would serve as symbols of the last time he ever let Absalom use him. The next thing he noticed was that he was wearing nothing but boxers. He glanced up at Kerr and Thatcher and gestured to his current state. Kerr chuckled and told him he would go find him some clothes. He left the room, leaving Malcolm alone with Thatcher.

"So, what day is it?" Malcolm asked.

"It's actually Thanksgiving. We missed the big meal, but I'm sure there are plenty of leftovers for us to dig into once you're dressed. You've got to be hungry," Thatcher said.

"Thanksgiving? But when I left, it was the middle of September. How has it been that long?" Malcolm asked, trying to wrap his mind around the time he lost.

Kerr returned with some clothes, apologizing that they were likely to be too big. Malcolm shrugged his shoulders and put on the oversized t-shirt and sweatpants. He followed Thatcher and Kerr out of the room and started down the stairs. They heard laughter coming from the kitchen, telling them the rest of the group was cleaning up after the Thanksgiving meal.

As they entered the kitchen, Malcolm made eye

contact with Dorian. More memories came crashing back to him. He remembered the stories Absalom had told him the night he returned. He knew there were some important details he had to share.

"Thatcher!" Malcolm exclaimed.

"What?" Thatcher asked in surprise.

"I have to tell you about the night your parents died," he said seriously.

Chapter Thirty-Five:
Thatcher

Thatcher looked at Malcolm in disbelief as he told him what Absalom had shared with him. Thatcher didn't know how to react. He was angry at first, wondering why Malcolm had even brought up such painful memories. When he started his story, Thatcher felt like he couldn't breathe.

"It wasn't my fault," Thatcher said quietly.

Malcolm shook his head slowly. "No, he killed your family because of me. He killed them because I killed my mother."

"Malcolm! You did not kill your mother," Tahlia said firmly. "Every child of an Old Immortal born to a mortal woman has been motherless. You are no more responsible for that than you are for the actions Absalom took toward Thatcher's family."

"I know that in here," he said, pointing at his head. "But that's not how it feels here," he said, indicating his heart.

"Dorian, did you know my mother was your descendant?" Thatcher asked him.

"I found out a few years after they died. When I took

The Evolved

Nora in, I thought she was my last descendant. She was nine when your parents died," Dorian said, lost in his thoughts. "I remember her coming to me during the night sobbing. She told me she had a dream about a fire. She said she saw a little boy all alone watching his house burn, and knew his parents were inside. At the time, I thought it was just a dream."

"How did I know?" Nora whispered.

"I think she told you," Dorian said simply. "You kept telling me you saw a woman. The woman took you there. You had dreams after that, and you always saw the same little boy. You would tell me he was sad and lonely. I could see how much it hurt you to see him that way. You told me your mother wanted you to find him."

"My mother? I don't even remember her." Nora appeared to be in shock.

"I know. You saw a picture of her in the newspaper clippings I kept from your accident. The day you found it, you came running to me and told me that this was the woman from your dreams. I didn't know what to think of that, so I started to investigate," Dorian said.

"I'm trying to wrap my head around this," Thatcher said. "How did Nora see me?"

"Your mother had the ability to project herself into others' thoughts. I'm not sure how she managed to linger for so long, but she made a connection with Nora and didn't break it until we found you," Tahlia explained, then her face softened. "Your mothers were sisters."

Thatcher looked over at Nora. He hadn't really noticed the similarities before. Of course, he thought her defined cheekbones and round eyes resembled his mother, but he hadn't really noticed anything else. He smiled at her when she caught him staring. Everyone in the room had come to feel like family to him. He and Whitley acted like siblings, always teasing each other and trying to get the better of one another. Kerr was definitely the big brother he never had, just as Malcolm seemed like a little brother. Tahlia, Romulus, and Dorian all seemed like kindly aunts and uncles, and even Eric had taken on the guise of a distant relative. His feelings toward Hadley were different, but their connection had been instantaneous. That left Nora. She was just there. He liked her all right, but she was more disconnected. He didn't feel as close to her as he did the others.

"So, Nora is my cousin?" Thatcher asked carefully. "My real cousin."

Nora nodded at him and came over to his side. "I guess we've both had real family all along."

Thatcher put an arm around her and gave her a small squeeze. He was still in shock, it was a lot to take in. But the most important thing that stood out to him was that his parents didn't die because of him. It had pained him to hear that Absalom killed them and enjoyed watching them die. He was angry that he'd gone his whole life blaming himself, but his anger was no longer directed inward.

Absalom had unknowingly created the very force that would destroy him. Thatcher felt his chest tighten at the realization that they had gained the upper hand.

The Evolved

His anger towards Absalom was intense. He killed his parents, he killed Nora's parents, he killed Kerr's father, and he tortured Malcolm. All the doubts he had about his destiny disappeared in an instant.

"Your heart and mind are at odds. You must learn to accept the differences and choose the path that honors both. Do not be led astray by the appearance of innocence," Thatcher said out loud.

He was greeted by confused looks when he began laughing. He had figured it out. His heart had told him it was all his fault, that he deserved everything that happened to him because he killed his family. His mind told him there was nothing he could have done. His heart and mind were at odds. He had not let himself be led astray by Malcolm. But the part that really mattered was right now. Thatcher smiled widely as he realized he had chosen his path.

"I know what I'm going to do," Thatcher said simply. "And I know we're going to win."

He looked at everyone and realized how crazy he must seem, which only made him laugh again. This time, his laughter brought something else with it. He felt a vibration in his chest that continued to intensify as he laughed. He stopped laughing when he realized the vibration was making him glow. White light was bursting from his hands and feet. The shock on the faces around him told him they were just as clueless as he was. He rose in the air a few inches, feeling the power surge through him. In his mind, he saw Absalom fall to his knees, grabbing his chest and screaming in anguish.

As quickly as it began, it ended. Thatcher found himself standing in the kitchen, facing everyone. They all wore shocked expressions, except Malcolm. Malcolm looked satisfied—maybe even happy.

"Do you feel it?" Malcolm asked him excitedly.

"He's weaker," Thatcher said, still trying to catch his breath.

"He's angry," Malcolm replied.

Thatcher nodded his head. When he saw Absalom on his knees, he felt a surge of power enter his body.

"What just happened?" Hadley asked in awe.

"Thatcher has claimed his prophecy with absolute certainty," Romulus answered with respect and amazement.

As all eyes landed on Thatcher. He wasn't sure how to tell them what this meant. But he had to tell them, they had to be ready. He took a deep breath.

"We need to be ready. He's coming to us. The battle will happen the day after tomorrow."

Chapter Thirty-Six:
Whitley

It took them all a moment to register what Thatcher was telling them. Whitley thought they still had time. She reached over and took Hadley's hand. Her twin squeezed her tightly. Thatcher's words sent chills through her body that she couldn't explain. She glanced at her parents. Her father looked worried. He was still so new to all of this. He had jumped back when Thatcher began glowing. Tahlia took his hand to calm and reassure him. Whitley wasn't sure how Eric would adjust to all this.

Kerr had wrapped Nora into a strong hug. He had the most to lose in this battle. Nora was carrying the future in her womb. But if she had figured out her prophecy, why hadn't she had a glowing moment? Whitley felt deflated as she realized that figuring out the prophecy was only half of the puzzle. Romulus had said Thatcher claimed it. It could be years before Nora's baby showed them why he or she was the future of the Evolved. Everyone was stationary for a few moments before all hell broke loose.

"What do we need to do?" Malcolm asked bravely.

"Where will we fight?" Kerr asked, glancing at Nora.

Thatcher just shook his head. "I don't know. I don't

even know how I know that much. When the power surged in me, I saw Absalom. He was screaming. He felt me there, and when he looked at me, I just saw it."

"He'll come here. If we wait here, he will come here. We need to take the fight somewhere else. We need to have the element of surprise," Nora said with certainty.

"If he's coming to us the day after tomorrow, we need to draw him out tomorrow," Romulus said.

Dorian nodded in agreement and looked at Tahlia. Whitley knew the Virtues had been waiting for this moment for centuries. They were finally going to put an end to Absalom.

"Where do we take the fight?" Whitley asked.

"I have an idea," Nora said. "I can think of a place that will help us gain an edge on Silas. We need to go tonight."

Whitley smiled at Nora. She was so tough and in command.

"Okay, everyone gather what you'll need. Think simple, warm, and flexible. Be back here in twenty minutes. Nora will transport us all together," Dorian instructed.

In only a few moments, Thatcher, Nora, Kerr, Romulus, and Dorian had left the kitchen. Whitley stood, looking at her parents and sister. The realization that this could be the last time they were all together hit her very hard. Hadley felt her distress and pulled her into a hug. Their parents surrounded them, and they held onto each other for a few minutes.

"Everything will turn out the way it is supposed to," Tahlia reassured them.

Whitley nodded at her mother. "That's what I'm afraid of. We don't really know how it's supposed to turn out, do we? We are going up against a crazy Old Immortal who has made it his life goal to kill everyone who stands in his way. Guess what? We're standing in his way."

"Whitley, I've seen you use your abilities. You are kick-ass," Hadley said.

"Hadley!" Eric scolded.

"What? She is!" Hadley said innocently, giving Whitley a wink.

"I know. We're all great in theory, but are we really a match for Silas and Absalom?" Whitley asked.

"You heard Thatcher! We're going to win," Hadley exclaimed. Whitley admired her sister's faith in her boyfriend. She knew in the pit of her stomach that they were right; the Evolved were going to win. But it didn't make her less afraid.

"Whitley, do you remember when you were seven, and Hadley was rollerblading? She was practicing skating backward and rolled down the driveway," Eric said.

"Yes. She didn't see the car coming. But I did," Whitley replied.

"I remember seeing it in slow motion. You ran down the driveway and into the road. You pushed her out of the way, just as she rolled into the path of the car. You didn't think, you just did it," Eric told her in awe at the memory.

"I remember. You knocked me over, and we both landed on our sides. The impact fractured our collar bones. Yours on the left, mine on the right," Hadley told Whitley.

Whitley nodded. She knew what her father was telling her. She needed to be fearless. She needed to do what she could to stop this man, and she needed to protect her sister. She put on a brave face and nodded again.

"Thank you, daddy. I needed that," Whitley said.

The girls each hugged their father and told him they would see him soon. Eric smiled at them and told them he loved them. He surprised them both by grabbing their mother and pulling her into a deep kiss. The girls sighed simultaneously and grinned at their parents. Whitley grabbed Hadley by the arm and pulled her out of the room. Hadley started to pout but stopped when she realized Whitley was only giving their parents the appearance of privacy. They listened quietly from the dining room.

"I don't know if I can let you leave," Eric told Tahlia.

"I have to go. They need me. You need to wait here where you're safe," she told him.

"It's like I'm losing you again. Only this time, I might lose all of you, forever," he said quietly.

"You won't lose us. No matter what happens, we're always going to be here," Tahlia told him. Whitley knew she was pointing at his heart.

"Promise me something, Lia?" Eric asked.

"I can try, Eric. What is it?" Tahlia whispered.

"Come back to me this time," he pleaded.

Hadley let a small sob escape her as she hugged Whitley. Whitley was crying silently. She knew she needed to be strong for her sister and her parents. This was not the end for them. No matter what happened, Whitley would make sure her mother would come back to her father.

Chapter Thirty-Seven:
Nora

As she changed her clothes, she turned to see Kerr watching her. Nora blushed slightly but finished getting dressed silently. She walked up to him and wrapped her arms around his waist. Kerr rested his chin on top of her head and sighed.

"I don't want you to come with us," Kerr told her.

"I know. But you don't really get to decide that," Nora said sadly. "We already know I won't be in the thick of it. I'll be safely to the side."

It had been part of the plan to keep both Kerr and Nora out of the way, but, since Kerr had developed more useful abilities, he would be needed in the battle. It made her feel better knowing that Kerr would be there to help her family if they needed him, but it didn't keep her from fearing for his safety.

"I love you, Kerr," she said as she pulled away and looked into his eyes.

"I love you too, Nora." Kerr leaned down and kissed her gently.

Nora pulled him close to her and deepened the kiss. Kerr reached up and tangled his hands in her hair. They poured their souls into that kiss as though it would be their last. When they broke away, Kerr looked at her and smiled.

"I have something for you, but I'm not going to give it to you until it's over, and Absalom is gone," Kerr told her with a grin.

Nora shook her head and smiled back. She knew they would both make it; she had seen it in her dream. They were going to live, they were going to get married, and they were going to have a baby. She kissed him again.

"Oh, did I tell you I know what we're having?" he asked playfully.

"No! Tell me!" Nora exclaimed.

He leaned in closely and whispered in her ear, "A girl."

When he pulled away, he was grinning stupidly at her. She couldn't help but feel her heartbeat a little faster. How had she fallen so hard in such a short amount of time? She watched him pull on his t-shirt and grab a zip-up sweatshirt. She took his hand and transported them into the kitchen to find everyone else waiting for them.

"Alright, Nora, where are we going?" Dorian asked.

"To the warehouse where Thatcher killed Caprice," Nora said simply.

"Genius!" Thatcher said appreciatively.

Nora smiled at them all and took Kerr's hand. "Everyone ready?"

Within moments, they were standing in the middle of the empty lot. It was dark, but Nora could make out the warehouses surrounding them. She smiled at Thatcher as he released some of his power into the air. Soon, there were small orbs of light dancing above them.

"Alright, we need to get some things set up, make our battle plan," Nora said.

"Nora needs to be somewhere high where she can see the battle," Romulus said.

"There," Thatcher said, pointing to a broken-out window in one of the warehouses.

Nora nodded at Romulus, and they headed over to check it out. As they made their way up the stairs, Nora looked down at the Evolved. They had come so far. Everyone was ready for this battle. Dorian caught her eye and put his hand over his heart. She smiled and did the same.

Romulus reached the top of the stairs and pushed the door open. They walked into the large empty room and turned toward the window. Nora could see them all perfectly. She leaned forward and shouted that this would work.

Dorian sat down and began to meditate. He closed his eyes and began to call to Silas and Absalom. Now they had to wait.

Chapter Thirty-Eight:
The Battle

Kerr

"Look out!" Kerr shouted.

He had sensed them coming. He felt their anger roiling through the air. The next thing he knew, there was fire raining from the sky.

"Ahh! Ouch!" Hadley yelled out, gripping her shoulder. When she moved her hand away, Kerr saw the fabric had been burned away where she was hit.

Whitley threw a shield of energy above them, and the small fireballs disintegrated upon impact. Kerr looked around him at the other Evolved and the two Old Immortals on the ground with them. Glancing up, he saw Nora pull back into the window.

Malcolm and Thatcher stood at the front, Whitley stood behind them, and Hadley, Dorian, and Tahlia were standing with Kerr. He looked in the direction the fireball had come from and saw Absalom stalking out from between two warehouses. Kerr didn't have time to help Hadley.

"Silas is coming from behind," Nora said in his head.

He didn't have time to think, he called out to the

others to turn around. They turned with him to face Silas as he sent ice shards flying at them.

Tahlia

With a wave of her hand, Tahlia threw the force field up in front of them. The ice hit it and fell to the ground. The ground started rumbling under their feet as Silas called to the fault lines beneath the earth's surface. She watched Kerr out of the corner of her eye. He hadn't had time to hide before the appearance of Silas and Absalom. She silently hoped Nora would hide him from view to give him the chance to get out of the way. She felt her daughters behind her and knew they were divided. Hadley faced Silas, and Whitley was facing Absalom with Malcolm and Thatcher.

"He's going to split the battle," Kerr told her.

She nodded and prepared for the quake.

Thatcher

Absalom walked slowly toward them, his face full of predatory intent. Malcolm was to his right, both of them poised for an attack. The ground started shaking as he heard Whitley cry out behind him.

"Silas is splitting the battle," Nora told him.

He nodded his head to tell her he understood. Absalom came to a stop in front of them and looked between Thatcher and Malcolm.

"Aww, how sweet," Absalom said with venom in his voice. "You ran right back to the losing side, Malcolm."

"No, he came back to the sane side," Thatcher told him.

"Well, sanity isn't all it's cracked up to be," Absalom replied as he raised his arm and twisted it.

Malcolm began to choke. When he coughed, smoke came from his mouth.

Thatcher shot a stream of fire at Absalom, but he repeated the hand motion. Thatcher felt fire beginning in his belly and rising in his chest. He coughed violently, tasting the smoke. Soon both he and Malcolm were on the ground gasping for air.

Thatcher heard a groan and a thud. Instantly, the burning dissipated, and he took a gulp of air. Thatcher heard Malcolm gasping beside him. Sitting up, Thatcher glanced around and saw Whitley dusting off her jeans as she stalked away from Absalom. She gave Thatcher a wink as she helped Malcolm to his feet.

Thatcher shook his head at Malcolm as he took a step forward. "Don't be a hero, Malcolm."

Malcolm growled quietly. "I need to do this, Thatcher."

Malcolm

He took a step forward and faced the man who was supposed to be his father.

"I am not afraid of you," he said boldly.

"I beg to differ," Absalom taunted. "I seem to remember a significant amount of whimpering over the last few months."

The Evolved

"Pain does that to someone," Malcolm retorted. "I'm sure you did your fair share of whimpering when you realized you'd dealt my mother a death sentence."

Absalom gave him a pained look, which was quickly taken over by a sneer. "You think you can hurt my feelings, boy? You have no idea who you're dealing with."

"I know exactly who I'm dealing with. That is why I returned to the Evolved. You are a hollow shell. You breed hatred and suffering wherever you go. You never loved my mother; you were just obsessed with her. You are not capable of love," Malcolm said, feeling his voice growing louder and stronger as he did.

"Love? That's what you think this is about?" Absalom asked with incredulity. "I've walked this earth for centuries. I've been cast to the side and banished by the one being that was supposed to love *me*. Love doesn't last. The only thing that lasts is power."

Malcolm was about to respond when he heard Whitley yawn loudly beside him. "I'm bored," she said.

Malcolm and Thatcher laughed, leaving Absalom enraged.

Absalom threw his arms out, surrounding them with a wall of fire. The heat reverberated back at them, the flames moving with his laughter. Malcolm realized he was actually terrified. This wasn't a game. Absalom wasn't going to mess around this time. He was here to kill them. All of them.

Whitley

As soon as the fire wall went up, a horrifying sound filled the air, like the earth was ripping apart. She turned just in time to shove Hadley as the ground split between them. Whitley looked across the opening into her sister's eyes. That was close—too close for comfort. What was even more terrifying was that they were now divided, and the fissure was too wide to jump across. The words of their prophecy played through her mind in the few seconds she stared at her sister.

Although you are the same, you may go in different directions. But your greatest strengths appear when you are as one.

Whitley furrowed her brow as she considered their current predicament. Right now, they were heading in different directions. Hadley had turned to face Silas just before he attacked, and Whitley was turning back to fight Absalom. Even with this short of a distance between them, she felt an emptiness inside her. When they were together, they were stronger, they were in tune. But when they were apart, something was missing.

Whitley snapped back to reality just in time to see Absalom use one of his acquired abilities to launch a steel pipe at Malcolm. It was too late to put up a shield, so Whitley focused on the pipe. At the last minute, it split in two, continuing its trajectory on either side of Malcolm.

The Evolved

Dorian

Dorian looked next to him, where Kerr had been standing just moments before. He was gone. The ground had split open, and Kerr was gone. It hit him hard just thinking about the possibility that they'd lost one of the Evolved so quickly. He pushed the thought from his mind in order to keep his focus. He tried not to panic as he whipped his head around, looking for him.

Silas had thrown ice shards at them and attempted a physical attack on Hadley. The thunder began to roll overhead, and lightning struck the ground next to Silas. The wind whipped around them, and Silas nodded appreciatively.

"Nicely done," Silas taunted. "I can't wait to add that to my repertoire."

Silas attacked. The water poured from his hands, freezing as it came. Taking aim at Hadley, he was taken off guard when his assault backfired. A blizzard whipped around Silas in an instant. Dorian could see him desperately trying to pull back his ability so the freezing onslaught would end. When Silas finally regained control, he tried a different approach.

Dorian tried to shout a warning, but it was too late. Tahlia was struck by a spear of ice. Dorian knew he couldn't kill them, but the distraction would be enough for Hadley to let her guard down. If only he knew where Kerr had gone.

Nora

Romulus was tense. Nora kept looking at him because she knew how badly he wanted to join the fight. No one was moving. It was like watching a deadly game of chicken, each side waiting for the other to strike first. Something was changing. A subtle shift in Dorian's body language told her something was going to happen.

She watched as Tahlia gathered her energy and shot at Silas like a bullet. Her heart was in her throat as Tahlia made contact with Silas. Romulus shifted his weight nervously.

"Go help them," Nora said simply.

"I can't. I need to stay with you," Romulus told her.

"I don't need a babysitter, Romulus. I'm safe here. They need you," Nora replied stubbornly.

She could see the inner struggle he was going through. He needed help in making up his mind. She punched him in the arm and transported him inside the fire wall.

"Ouch," he exclaimed, then took in his surroundings.

Nora gave him a stern look. "Go." Then she transported herself back inside the warehouse.

Hadley

Hadley watched in horror as her mother fell to the ground. The spear of ice was sticking out of her abdomen.

The Evolved

"Mom!" Hadley screamed. She ran over to her side, letting the wind die in an instant. Romulus had appeared and was trying to pull her away from her mother.

"Hadley, listen to me," Romulus yelled over the roar of the fire.

"We can't lose her. If she's gone, there's no hope," Hadley yelled back.

Romulus shook his head at her and smiled. "Remember, only the Evolved can kill an Old Immortal. You will not lose your mother today."

Hadley suddenly understood. Only she could defeat Silas. She couldn't worry about her mother or the other Virtues.

"You three need to get out of the way. You're too much of a distraction, and you're essentially useless to us right now," Hadley told Romulus.

He looked hurt, but she knew he understood. This wasn't training, this was war.

She whipped her head around to the other side of the battle and saw Thatcher and Absalom exchanging fire while Whitley attempted to block the fatal blows. Absalom was planning something. He could have easily killed them by now. She looked at Romulus and grinned.

"Tut-tut looks like rain!" Hadley yelled as the rain fell in sheets.

The sudden downpour surprised Absalom enough that he lost control of the flames. As soon as the flames disappeared, she stopped the rain. Pulling back, Hadley prepared to take Silas on by herself.

She struck him with lightning as she ran toward him. He yelped at the shock but responded quickly. Hadley dodged a large ice spear as he shot it at her, only to be caught by a few smaller volleys he sent her way. Hadley pushed the pain out of her mind. She had a burned shoulder and cuts on her face and side. She didn't have time to wonder where Kerr was as she prepared for the next attack.

She threw a few more lightning bolts at Silas as she ran toward him. When she got close enough, she gathered the lightning and punched him in the face. He fell to the ground from the shock.

"Whoop!" Hadley yelled, bouncing on the ground. She turned to see how the other Evolved were fairing. Three to one, and they were barely making a dent in Absalom. She started to run toward the crater between the battles but stopped short when her sister flung herself across the gap.

"Hadley, look out!" Malcolm yelled, pointing behind her.

Whitley

She watched in disbelief as an ice wall formed behind Hadley. Her sister turned toward them. Hadley thought she'd won. What an idiot! The ice wall began moving closer to her. Inch by inch, Hadley was being pushed into the chasm in front of her.

Whitley was moving in an instant. Thatcher tried to block her when he realized what she was doing, but she barreled him over. The only thought in her mind was getting to Hadley. After closing the distance between her and the gaping hole in the ground, she launched herself into the air. As she collided with her sister, she found herself face to face with her mother.

Looking around her, she saw nothing but white. She was in a bright expanse that seemed limitless.

"Whitley," Tahlia said breathlessly.

"Mom?" Whitley answered.

"I knew this moment would come. I knew it would come to this," Tahlia said sadly. "You chose to sacrifice yourself for your sister."

"Is that what happened?" Whitley asked. "I just knew I couldn't let her die."

Tahlia nodded. "When faced with the possibility of her death, you chose to sacrifice your life for hers. Your prophecy has been fulfilled."

"So, you're saying I'm dead?" Whitley asked her mother.

"No, you're not dead, you've just finally become one and embraced the fullest extent of your abilities," Tahlia replied.

Whitley closed her eyes to fight back the tears that threatened to fall. She knew she was making the right decision when she launched herself at her sister. She didn't hesitate for a single second because she knew it was time. Now she was standing in front of her mother, essentially being told that she was never going to exist outside of this white expanse again. She would never see her sister again, and she would never be able to laugh with her again. She would never see her father become President, or witness the reunion of her parents.

"Hadley . . . Dad. . . Mom," Whitley cried, turning her attention to her mother.

"Oh, Whitley, I'm so sorry," Tahlia told her as she enfolded her daughter in her arms. "I only just got my family back. I love you, Whitley. Never forget that."

Whitley let go of her mother and walked away. When she turned around, Tahlia was gone, and she was alone.

Nora

Whitley was gone. She had watched as Whitley dove at her sister and didn't come out on the other side. Nora tried desperately to reach her through telepathy, but there was no response. Nora tried to concentrate on Whitley to take herself to her, but she was gone.

Nora choked back a sob and reached out to Romulus.

"Whitley is gone," Nora told him.

"What do you mean, gone?" Romulus' voice echoed in her mind.

"I mean . . . " Nora couldn't finish the sentence. Her heart was breaking.

"No!" Romulus yelled in her mind.

"You need to get out of there. If Thatcher or Hadley inadvertently hit you with their abilities, you will die.

The Evolved

Bring Dorian and Tahlia with you," Nora told him.

Nora knew Romulus would see the logic in her instructions, but she didn't look away until she was certain they were heading up to her. She looked back down at the fight. None of the Evolved had sustained any serious injuries, but the fight was only just getting started. The door burst open, and Dorian came in with Romulus carrying an unconscious Tahlia in his arms.

"I can't leave her. She needs me!" Tahlia cried as she opened her eyes.

"Tahlia, you know you will only be in the way. You're injured, you need to rest," Dorian told her calmly.

Nora looked away from her aunt. She couldn't handle the grief right now. She needed to focus on the battle. Kerr was near Malcolm, helping him anticipate Absalom's next move. She had cloaked him from the Old Immortals, but the other Evolved could still see him. He had already helped Malcolm avoid a few narrow misses from Absalom. She looked down at Hadley, urging her to wake up before Silas gained the upper hand.

Hadley

She felt something slam into her back. As she fell, she was momentarily disoriented. A vibration began at the base of her spine and spread slowly through her whole body. She felt herself being lifted off the ground. She opened her eyes and was no longer in the battle. She was in a white room that seemed never-ending. The silence was deafening. She turned around and her breath caught in her chest. She saw Whitley, and she was crying.

They stood facing each other for a moment before they both started talking at once.

"Where are . . . " Hadley began.

"Hadley, listen . . . " Whitley began.

Hadley gestured for her sister to go first.

"Had, we don't have much time. You need to get back to the battle," Whitley told her.

"What about you?" Hadley asked with uncertainty.

"I'm not going back. I can't. Do you remember what mom told us after our prophecy?" Whitley asked, sadly.

"That we were two halves of a whole. Just like we've always said." Hadley didn't understand.

"That's right. And our prophecy identifies us as the divided. One being divided in two. In order to win this fight, one of us had to go back." Whitley forced the words out. "I chose me. I love you so much, and I can't imagine living without you. We can't both survive this, Had. You have to survive. You have to win."

"Whitley, no." Hadley felt like she'd been punched in the stomach.

"You know this is how it had to be. I need you to understand. As soon as I saw you fighting Silas, I knew. I knew in my gut that you needed me. You didn't need me to fight next to you, you needed me to be part of you so you could fight," Whitley cried.

Hadley didn't want to accept it. She didn't want to be

left without her sister. Without her best friend. How was she supposed to go on knowing that her twin would never be with her again? The light began to dim, leaving Hadley to understand that the choice had been made for her. She looked in her sister's eyes and pulled her into a hug.

"I love you, Whitley."

"I love you, Hadley."

When she opened her eyes, she was back in the battle, and she was glowing. She saw Thatcher throw a fireball as she fell to the ground.

Thatcher

Thatcher watched helplessly as Hadley crumpled to the ground again.

"Hadley, you have to get up," he whispered.

"Nora, she has to get up. Tell her," he pleaded.

The rain was pouring, and the wind was picking up. Thatcher knew Hadley realized her sister was gone. She had to pull herself together and use her anger for the right reasons. He smiled sadly as Hadley slowly stood and turned to face Silas.

"She will be alright. She got to say goodbye," Nora cried in his mind.

Thatcher looked over at Malcolm. He knew he needed his help. All the kid could do was fly. He tore himself away from his thoughts and threw another lava ball at Absalom.

"Thatcher, it's rude to interrupt father/son time like that," Absalom said coldly.

"Tahlia was right, you do like to play with your food," Thatcher said sardonically.

"Hmm, well, she's not wrong. It's more fun if I toy with you first," Absalom said, sending out a flame that burned Thatcher's leg.

He cried out in pain, but couldn't bring himself to break eye contact with Absalom. He knew this was just one of his games. He wanted Thatcher to look away, so he maintained eye contact.

"You're a coward, Absalom. You are so wrapped up in yourself that you can't handle that someone else could be more powerful than you," Thatcher said.

"Oh yes, now comes the pointless banter. How about we skip that part, and I kill you all?" Absalom said.

"That would be ideal, but it never seems to happen, now does it?" Thatcher threw back at him.

Absalom had begun to circle around him slowly like a panther stalking its prey. He and Malcolm both turned to face him at each new angle.

"Do you know what's down there?" he asked, pointing toward the cavity Silas had created. "Heat. Fire. The core of the Earth."

Thatcher didn't know where this was going, but he didn't think it would end well. He was now facing the other side of the battle. He realized the rain had stopped, and the wind had died down again, but from the intensity with which Hadley was fighting Silas,

The Evolved

Thatcher knew this was the calm before the storm.

Hadley

As Hadley stood up, she could feel the difference. For the first time in her life, she didn't feel like she needed anyone. She had to regain her bearings. She could feel the power building inside of her as Whitley's half joined hers. It was a strange sensation and left her feeling slightly disoriented. She strode to Silas and began engaging him in hand to hand combat. She was angry and needed to take it out on him. Silas fought like a girl. He had clearly gotten used to using his abilities to intimidate and murder.

"Hey, let's play a game," Hadley said to Silas. "I'm sure you've heard of electroshock therapy? Well, it's not really a common thing anymore, because it's all cruel and unusual . . . But I think it would be perfect for you. Mostly because you're also cruel and unusual."

Silas was confused for a moment, so she decided to just show him what she had in mind. One after another, Hadley pummeled him with bolts of electricity. He shook and convulsed each time she struck him. Now that she was no longer divided, she was able to tap into both the weather and the energy around her. She was fast, and she was resourceful.

Silas sent another ice spear soaring toward her. Holding up a hand, Hadley suspended it in air, then she spun it around a few times before splitting it into hundreds of tiny shards. With a smile, she sent the shards soaring back toward Silas. He cried out as each shard sliced at his skin.

"I think you're playing for the wrong side, little girl," Silas said as blood dripped from the tiny cuts.

"Don't ever question what side I belong on," Hadley replied, holding both hands up. She called a lightning bolt and struck him down.

He whimpered from the pain. Hadley walked up to him and smiled slightly.

"That was from me. But, this is from Whitley."

She sent currents of energy through him. He convulsed on the ground. She caused every cell in his body to explode, one by one. For a moment, she enjoyed his screams of pain. All the people he had killed, all the pain he had caused, and all the moments she would miss her sister seemed to make his prolonged torture worth it. Then, because she knew she was full of light, she sent one last burst of energy through him, and he disintegrated in front of her.

Malcolm

Absalom was getting desperate. He saw his brother fall and was not going to let that happen to him. But Malcolm knew that Silas was nothing compared to Absalom. Silas was just a lackey. Absalom only kept him around to be his errand boy. Once Caprice had died, Silas was all but useless anyway.

Malcolm knew Absalom could take them all out in a matter of seconds, but he wanted to mess with Thatcher.

"He's scared, Malcolm. He sees that he can be taken down too. Now that all of us are focused on him, he is going to get more ruthless," Kerr whispered next to him.

Malcolm had only survived this long in the fight because Kerr helped him understand and determine what Absalom was feeling. Malcolm nodded his head to let Kerr know he understood. He didn't want to draw too much attention to Kerr. If Absalom knew he was there, he would be in danger.

Thatcher and Malcolm were now facing the panicked Absalom with the absolute certainty that this would be the end. The wind began to pick up again as Hadley came to join them. She would let them end it, but she wanted to help. Absalom turned his attention to Hadley. She was the one he could gain the most power from at this point.

The sides of his mouth twisted into a wicked smile as he shot a fireball at Hadley, only to have it deflect and hit him in the side. He hissed in pain and sent another volley in her direction. She stood with her arms crossed behind an energy shield, and another round shot back at Absalom, this time striking him in the leg. He howled in anger at the look of boredom on her face.

"Really? Picking on a girl?" Thatcher taunted.

Absalom was done playing games. He crouched low, seeming to pull the liquid fire out of the ground. He stood up holding two balls of lava in his hands. There was no warning. In an instant, the lava was flying at Thatcher. Time seemed to slow. He heard Hadley's raw scream, he saw Kerr rush forward, and he heard Nora gasp in his mind.

Malcolm made a split-second decision.

Thatcher

The lava was heading straight for him. He didn't have a chance to react. This was it. He looked at Hadley to his right. The grief was already present on her face, but something zipped past him, and the impact never came.

"Argh!" Thatcher cried out and fell to his knees as he felt a surge of power and strength enter him. He looked to his left and saw Malcolm lying on the ground with smoke rolling out of his chest. Kerr was on his knees beside the lifeless body. Thatcher knew it was too late.

The lightning flashed in the sky, and the thunder boomed overhead. Hadley had joined him just in time.

"Get. Them. Out. Nora," he yelled each word as the rage bubbled over.

He took Hadley's hand. Their power connected, and the storm picked up. Fire, lightning, and energy crackled in the air. They were enveloped in a whirlwind of power. Thatcher looked around him and realized the moment had come; he looked at Hadley and squeezed her hand before releasing it.

The fire in the vortex dissipated when he lost contact with Hadley. Hadley stepped back, giving Thatcher room to take care of Absalom.

When Thatcher saw how Absalom looked at them, he was disgusted. Absalom's face was full of awe and hunger. He envied their abilities.

The Evolved

"You know, Thatcher, we could have a good life. If you join me now, your little girlfriend can come too. I've taken a bit of a liking to her," Absalom yelled.

"I would rather die," Thatcher told him.

"I can arrange that. There's no one left that is stupid enough to jump in front of you to save your life. Malcolm was a waste of space," Absalom said as he spat on the ground.

Thatcher felt the heat in his gut rise and spread through his body. Not only had Absalom killed Malcolm, but he was also trying to belittle him. Thatcher thrust his hand forward, and a beam of light shot from it. He was momentarily taken aback before he realized what it meant. Malcolm died. Absalom now only shared his abilities with Thatcher.

Thatcher smiled as the realization sank into his mind. Every descendant of the Old Immortals Absalom killed had their ability taken from them. Now, each of those abilities was coursing through his body as well as Absalom's.

He glanced over his shoulder. Everyone was gone, even Hadley. He hadn't noticed the storm die around him. Absalom looked at him with unrestrained malice.

"They've all left you. They left you here, all alone. Is that the kind of family you always wanted?" Absalom taunted him.

Thatcher ignored his comment and smiled at him. "You know, this isn't going to be that difficult."

"What's this? You discover some new superpower and

you think that means you have the upper hand?" Absalom asked wickedly.

"It gives me a fighting chance," Thatcher told him. "Because now I can do everything you can."

Absalom lunged at Thatcher, his body igniting into a human flame. Thatcher dove out of the way, listening to Absalom laugh as he landed. He realized that even though he now had the same abilities as Absalom, he had no idea what they were or how to use them all.

"Neat trick," Thatcher said, trying to sound unimpressed.

Absalom laughed louder and threw another lava ball at Thatcher. Instinct kicked in as Thatcher reached up and caught the lava in his hands before throwing it back at Absalom. He was pleased to see the look of surprise in his enemy's eyes as the lava struck his arm. Thatcher couldn't believe that worked. He simply decided the lava wouldn't burn him because he could use it too, and it didn't. Absalom was no idiot. Thatcher had to move quickly before Absalom caught on to his thought process.

Taking a few steps back, Thatcher found himself stumbling over something in his path. He landed on the ground with his legs on top of the obstruction he'd fallen over. The smell was unmistakable and took him back to the night his parents died. Burning flesh. To his horror, he had tripped over the body that used to be Malcolm. He found himself looking into the staring eyes of the thirteen-year-old who had been tortured and killed because he went against his father. The pain in his chest intensified as his eyes traveled down to the gaping hole in Malcolm's abdomen. This boy did not deserve to die.

Jumping up, Thatcher put all his focus on Absalom. He narrowed his eyes and smiled slightly as he saw Absalom grab onto his chest. Right about then, Absalom was feeling his airways constrict as the oxygen in his lungs turned to smoke. Thatcher pushed more emotion into his ability and felt a sense of satisfaction as Absalom fell to his knees. Absalom looked into Thatcher's eyes with anger and confusion. He didn't understand how Thatcher was winning.

"You see, Absalom," Thatcher said as he crouched down in front of him, "you made the mistake of killing people I care very deeply for. First, my parents. Now, Malcolm. Not to mention all the people you killed who meant something to the people I now consider my family."

Absalom coughed, trying to speak, but Thatcher had heard enough of his brand of bull.

"I think now is the time for you to listen, Absalom." Thatcher leaned in a little closer. "Do you know why you won't win this? I'll tell you. Because you're fighting for the wrong reasons."

Absalom fell to his hands and knees. His face was red with the effort he was putting into each breath. He groaned as Thatcher turned the heat up inside his body.

"I am fighting for the future. You are fighting to regain the past. I am fighting for those I love. You are fighting because you hate everyone but yourself," Thatcher told him, leaning close to Absalom's face.

Thatcher watched Absalom struggle for a few more moments. He had had enough of this shell of a man. He released his lungs, allowing him to gulp in much-needed oxygen. Then, with a flick of his wrist, Thatcher raised Absalom's body temperature. His scream echoed through Thatcher's very core. It was angry, it was pained, and it was full of disbelief. Thatcher watched as Absalom convulsed a few times before falling to the ground.

An eerie sound filled the air as black tendrils of smoke rose from the body in front of Thatcher. They spiraled up to form a black ball above Absalom. The sound was deafening, like every soul destroyed by Absalom had been released. Thatcher took a step back as the ball began to vibrate and glow. As the glow intensified, the color faded from the dark black of Absalom's soul to a blinding white. Shielding his eyes, Thatcher peered out around him. For just a moment, he saw the faded silhouettes of every soul Absalom had taken, and he felt the relief and gratitude emanating from each of them. Then all at once, they were gone. The glowing ball was now levitating in front of Thatcher, and it crackled with energy before it merged with his body.

Chapter Thirty-Nine:
Nora

Nora had transported them all back to the house, leaving Hadley and Thatcher to face Absalom alone. Dorian and Romulus were both pacing the library. They knew Thatcher was destined for this, but they didn't know what condition he would be in when he returned. Tahlia had left them in the library to tell Eric about Whitley alone.

"Hadley is calling to me," Nora said as she jumped to her feet and disappeared.

She reappeared near the warehouse. Hadley was standing off to the side, nervously watching Thatcher. She took Nora's hand and nodded at her. Nora transported them back into the library.

Dorian stopped pacing and looked relieved when he saw both of them. He smiled sadly at Hadley. Nora knew he wanted to say something to her, but he couldn't find the right words. He stepped forward and gingerly wrapped his arms around Hadley. He released her and kissed her forehead.

Kerr stepped forward to heal her wounds. She had been burned on her shoulder and had a few other scrapes and bruises from the fight. As soon as she was healed, she sat down and began to cry.

"I can't believe she's gone." Hadley sobbed, finally letting the loss of her sister wash over her.

Nora held her as they cried together. Dorian tore his eyes away from them to look at Romulus. His brother was talking to Kerr quietly in the corner. Dorian knew the two of them were experiencing and seeing all the loss Hadley felt. Even though they didn't experience it firsthand, they were feeling her pain and doubt and confusion.

"I left Thatcher alone with Absalom. Absalom has been weakened, but he will still put up one hell of a fight. Please let me know when Thatcher returns," Hadley told them before she excused herself and went in search of her parents.

Nora sat down next to Kerr and took his hand in hers. She gave him a sad smile and waited. She didn't have to wait long before she felt that pull in her stomach again. Thatcher was calling to her. She closed her eyes and went to him.

When she arrived, he was sitting on the ground next to Malcolm. Nora walked over and sat down next to him. He was crying and holding onto Malcolm's hand. Nora looked at the body of the boy who had sacrificed himself for the Evolved. If she just looked at his face, she could see the boy she met in the skate park. But as her eyes traveled down his body she saw the gaping hole in his chest. Malcolm did not deserve this. He did not deserve to die, especially at the hands of his own father. Nora put her arm around Thatcher and sat with him for a few moments.

"We should bring his body back," she told him.

"Do you think Dorian would let us bury him? He deserves a proper funeral," Thatcher said.

Nora nodded her head and took hold of both Malcolm and Thatcher. She took them to the back patio where they left Malcolm's still form. They made their way in the back door, through the breakfast nook, and down the hall to the library.

Kerr came forward and healed the burns on Thatcher's body. Thatcher thanked him and went on to explain what had happened in the battle. Nora was in awe of his strength and determination. She was so proud of him. If it weren't for Thatcher, Hadley, and Whitley, they wouldn't have been victorious.

"It's over. I realized what the difference between us was, and I used it to my advantage," Thatcher told them all.

The library door opened as Tahlia and Eric walked in. Hadley pushed past them and rushed at Thatcher. He pulled her to him and gave her a gentle kiss, resting his forehead against hers. She blinked back the tears and nodded at him before hugging him tightly. Kerr and Nora came forward. The four of them hugged each other in relief. Nora knew the coming days would not be easy, but they had each other. They had made it.

Chapter Forty:
Dorian

After the millennia they had been waiting for this battle, Dorian couldn't help but wonder what would be coming next. He knew this battle was only part of ushering in the New Era. Absalom and Silas had been standing in their way, but they weren't the only obstacle the Evolved were going to have to overcome. Everything Absalom represented was about to be eradicated from the world. The evil he held, the havoc he wreaked, and the corruption he caused would be gone with him.

As wonderful as a world without the cause of evil sounded, Dorian knew it would not be an easy transition. So many people had been living their lives clouded by the malevolent presence of Absalom, and they may not know what to do in a world devoid of that malevolence. The longer someone draws that wickedness into their being, the more it becomes an integral part of them. New threats would rise, and the Evolved would have to continue to fight until the final pieces of the prophecy fell into place. He glanced over at Nora and Kerr. Their child would play a key part in the New Era. It had been up to Hadley, Whitley, and Thatcher to end this battle, but it was up to Nora and Kerr to bring new hope to the world.

The Evolved

They were preparing for the burial of Malcolm. Thatcher had insisted on digging the grave. He had to heat the ground in order to thaw it out enough to dig. Kerr and Romulus had constructed a casket for him. They were going to bury Malcolm in the backyard. Nora had chosen the spot specifically for him. In the large garden, there was a gathering of lilac bushes, and in the middle of these bushes there was a small clearing. It wasn't much to look at during November in South Dakota, but it was breathtaking in the summer.

Dorian led the way as Kerr and Thatcher carried the casket. Hadley, Nora, Tahlia, and Eric followed behind them. When they arrived in the clearing, they set the casket on a bench. Each of them approached the casket and said their final goodbyes. Thatcher was the last to come forward. Dorian saw the tears in his eyes as he looked down at the young boy who had sacrificed himself so that Thatcher may live. Thatcher was clutching something to his chest as the tears ran down his cheeks. Dorian knew what it was before he watched Thatcher place it in the casket next to Malcolm.

Steggie. Thatcher closed his eyes as the tears spilled down his cheeks. He reached out and touched Malcolm's head and whispered something meant only for the two of them. Then Dorian stepped forward to say a few words.

"The Creator sent this boy to us. Absalom may have been his father, and he may have spared his life for dark purposes, but the bottom line is, the Creator knew we needed to be touched by Malcolm. He showed us that even though we think we know what to expect, we can always be surprised. He showed us that even though we've been raised to believe one thing, we have the power to believe something else. But most of all, Malcolm showed us the true meaning of sacrifice. He died to save the people he had been taught were the enemy. He died to ensure that we would be able to usher in the New Era. Malcolm will not be forgotten. He will be a part of us for the rest of our lives."

Dorian stepped back and watched as Kerr and Romulus closed the casket. They lowered him into the ground slowly and carefully. They all stayed in the clearing until Thatcher had finished refilling the grave. The Old Immortals and Eric walked back to the house, leaving the Evolved to pay their respects.

Despite their losses, they were supporting each other and showing the depths of their love for one another. He felt pride in how far they had come, and a sense of completion as the first part of the struggle was behind them. From the back patio, he saw Nora whisper something to Hadley as she hugged her tight. Kerr smiled at Thatcher and pulled him into a strong hug. Lying a hand on Thatcher's shoulder, Dorian saw the look that passed between them and knew they would handle anything that came their way.

Epilogue

"You need to hurry up!" Thatcher said as he hung up the phone.

He turned back to Hadley, who was nervously biting her nails. Eric sat in the corner with Tahlia sleeping on his shoulder. Dorian and Romulus were pacing the hospital waiting room.

"Is he on his way?" Hadley asked Thatcher.

"Yes. He said he was almost here. I can't believe he's not here already," Thatcher told her as he took her hand in his.

This wasn't the first time Kerr had been late for an important occasion. Thatcher practically had to send out a search party for him on his wedding day. He found Kerr nervously repeating his vows in the bathroom, but he made it to the front of the church with only a second to spare.

Thatcher shook his head and chuckled at the memory as Kerr came crashing through the elevator door.

"What room is she in?" he asked them breathlessly.

Kerr smiled at his family in the waiting room before he took off down the hallway. Hadley laughed as he ran.

The Evolved

"I can't believe this day is finally here," Hadley said as she squeezed Thatcher's hand.

Hadley had been through so much in the last year. Losing Whitley cut her to the core. She knew it was how things were supposed to be, and she knew her sister would always be with her. But it didn't make the loss any easier. Her parents had leaned on each other to deal with the loss. She looked over at her father as he absentmindedly played with Tahlia's hair. Hadley smiled at him when he caught her watching him.

She had made it through with the help of the other Evolved. Thatcher was amazing, even as he dealt with losing Malcolm, and Kerr had proven to be an emotional confidant for them both. Nora had become her best friend in the absence of Whitley. She knew with absolute certainty that everything had turned out exactly how it was supposed to.

Kerr took a deep breath and walked in the door. He gave Nora an apologetic shrug as he came to her side. He took her hand and kissed it.

"You can do this, Nora. It's time to meet our little girl," he whispered in her ear.

Nora nodded at him. Her water had broken that morning as she stepped out of the shower. She hadn't been expecting the baby to come for another week, so she felt a slight panic as she dressed and grabbed her hospital bag. She transported herself down to the kitchen, where she found everyone eating breakfast. At the sight of her holding her duffle bag and beaming from ear to ear, the whole family went into a frantic rush to get her to the hospital. Kerr had been at the

Benton Book Nook when they called him.

Another contraction hit her, and she started to push. The pressure was almost unbearable, but she knew it meant she would meet her little girl soon. Taking a deep breath, she gave another strong push and felt the small head leave her body. Her legs shook as the nurses told her to push one more time.

A small cry filled the room. The doctor handed her the small life that she'd been waiting to meet. Looking up at Kerr, she was overwhelmed with love as she saw the awe etched in his face through the tears swimming in her eyes. She looked into those impossibly large green eyes and knew the world would never be the same.

Acknowledgments

To Ryan, for putting up with my intense focus during the writing process. I know it hasn't been easy, but I am eternally grateful. I love you.

To mom & dad, for always believing in me and offering me the encouragement and feedback that has led me to this point.

To my mother-in-law, for the best birthday present ever.

To Missy, always remember the computer's flying at high tide.

To my little princess and my crazy little man, for seeing me as perfect and amazing even when I'm focused on other things. I love you both.

About the Author

KT Webb is a multi-genre indie author with a twisted sense of humor. When asked to describe herself, she generally tells people she's awkward AF and likely to say some really weird shit. KT isn't the kind of person you put on speakerphone, and you should probably monitor her caffeine intake.

When she isn't writing, KT can be found binge-watching serial killer documentaries on Netflix, goofing off with her two children, annoying her husband, going on adventures with her best friend, or snuggling her three kitties (Loki, Coal & Blaze).

Do not trust KT with sharp objects or adulty things

www.ingramcontent.com/pod-product-compliance
Lightning Source LLC
Chambersburg PA
CBHW022018240626
47154CB00007B/2159